S0-AVC-250

HURRY ALONG

HURRY ALONG

Sarah Plimpton

𝄞

PLEASURE BOAT STUDIO
New York

Copyright © 2012 by Sarah Plimpton

All rights reserved. This book may not be reproduced, in whole or part, in any form, except by reviewers, without the written permission of the publisher.

Hurry Along
by Sarah Plimpton

ISBN 978-1-929355-77-8
Library of Congress Control Number: 2011941902

Design by The Grenfell Press
Cover etching by Sarah Plimpton

Two chapters were originally published in *Single Skies*, Living Hand #8, 1976 and *Sienese Shredder #2*, 2008.

Pleasure Boat Studio books are available through the following:
SPD (Small Press Distribution) Tel. 800-869-7553, Fax 510-524-0852
Partners/West Tel. 425-227-8486, Fax 425-204-2448
Baker & Taylor 800-775-1100, Fax 800-775-7480
Ingram Tel 615-793-5000, Fax 615-287-5429
Amazon.com and bn.com

and through
PLEASURE BOAT STUDIO: A LITERARY PRESS
www.pleasureboatstudio.com
201 West 89th Street
New York, NY 10024

Contact Jack Estes
Fax: 888-810-5308
Email: pleasboat@nyc.rr.com

For Bob

CHAPTER I

Come along hurry along.

His short fattish legs rubbed against each other in the heat, slowing down he bounced his ball, placing his shadow under those of the leaves of the trees, hiding it in the black shapes of the buildings. His mother hurried on, he stopped altogether. There was an apple on the sidewalk split open in the sun rotten on the inside, the flesh was brown under the crinkling skin, liquid and ready to flow. Stepping up he kicked the sagging form to hit the wall and run down wetting the burning stone. The seeds appeared, pinned to the cement surface by the sun, stuck in the glue of the stuff of the apple, turning already as it lost its water into a hard fibrous tissue. His foot lightly touched the wet bottoms of the other paper bags to disengage their fillings. The ripe apples fell to the pavement cracked on the impact and broken open to the sun melted into soft and pliable shapes.

The heat was too great. She should have left him at home sitting on a chair with his knees up knocking at the flies that dropped to the floor, their wings shrunken and useless. Mutated in the high temperatures and forced to walk they fed on the moisture that clung to the walls, vegetables and fruits. The mosquitoes came through the screens crawling through the squares that had been widened by a pencil pushed in and turned until the wire cut into the soft wood and made an indented ring. Their shadows larger than life size appeared on the ceilings and walls, the high whine swelled, his ear usually silent and small grew and dwarfed his head. He brought them out of the tube with his finger, dwindling in the light.

Behind his head a fan pushed a current of air down the back of his neck stiffening the damp shirt with cold. Drops of moisture covered the glass on the table wetting the inside of his hand, he went outside the window onto the lawn rolling on the grass under the swing collecting the ticks marked up like small seeds. Taking hold they blackened with blood throbbing on his skin bursting finally with the pressure and heat. Walking in through the door he rubbed the sores picked up a peach bit through it filling his mouth with the soft pink fur. At the piano he played pressing the notes down with his careful touch, a steady monotonous rhythm. The dog got up and left the room pushing open the screen door running out onto the grass rolling over thrown onto his feet ran along the fence and went through a hole. The piano stopped, the dog barked down the street, the maid came in the room and swept the floor. In front of the window, he forced his eye against the screen.

Outside no one was there. The lawn was black with pools of water evaporating and disappearing from one spot to another. The sky was hazy whitish and low down. Over the fence the fields extended just to the horizon, the trees lining their borders never converged. When they walked through the grass towards the end their legs tired as the edge receded and they stopped to spread out the picnic lying on the ground to while away the time. The grass was flattened down, the ants carried away the crumbs and they threw out the fruit pits to come up once they had gone. Pigeon flocks flew under the dark clouds turning and turning with no sound, the rain never came, in the late afternoons of the other summers, they would come in from the fields and enter the front door as the first drops began to fall.

He swung on the garden gate back and forth in the sultry afternoons listening to the squeak, shifting his weight for the maximum sound to offset the noise of the insects rasping in the heat. He swung in the afternoon breeze squinting his eyes blurring the landscape that turned before him. The long narrow slit opened out on the clouds torn and ripped by the violent gusts, the black holes let in the wind and the cold drafts picked off the moisture icing him up inside. His words came coughing up the throat rolled in the mouth thrown off the palate they somersaulted out with ease, trailed with strings to be pulled in again if he felt the need. A collapsible ship launched on the sea, blown up with air floated easily on the heavy swell never drowned.

The sailboat started out across a cement pond catching the gusts of wind and heeling over pointing up into the wind, luffing and falling off again, he leaned over with his stick and sent it around to go back in the other direction, balanced on the gate and sent out a bubble without a string. It drifted in the wind, the colored liquid turning around and around, a stronger breath of wind came and carried it away. He wrinkled his forehead and sharpened his eye as it disappeared from his sight blowing out towards the fields into a void where it could expand to a size unseen, stretched out into an infinite number of shapes, where his words echoed and the light turned back on itself and started again.

The maid moved up behind flicking her dust cloth. Out she said, turning her back to his sudden stare and she emptied an ashtray tapping it into the fireplace.

His fingers stuck between the piano keys, expanded in the dampness. She had placed a tulip in a vase, the long stem whirled around the glass came to a stop, the bell opened out toward the boy. He looked down into its red cup with the yellow splotch at the end, at the yellow projections which extended toward him. Taking both hands he peeled the petals back turning them down against the long green succulent stem, bent his face close in, bit off the yellow stalks, rose up and left.

The buildings down the street hung from their roofs in the heat, little boys played endless games which they never scored, which never ended. The heat stayed on in the evening, they continued to play until the ball faded in the light, rolled along the ground unnoticed, disappeared into the shadow of the fence or into the darkened sky. Their cries in the end lost their force vanishing over the wall, they sat with their backs against the bench, their feet stretched out before them breathing deeply tapping the bats on the toes of their shoes. The sand blew whirling up behind the bases, the moon that rose up between the buildings was fat, orange and quiet.

Play ball?

Sometime.

The other heads turned his way down the bench, the ferrets

came out of their holes to look at the prey running close its white paws flashing in the failing light. His dog ran along the road his tongue out dripping swinging at the end flicking off drops of sweat, boiling up and rising high cutting, through the flower beds. Their muscles were tensed strung up tight.

Try us sometime kid.

Forget it.

They settled back down to wait. The moon rose higher, after a time they picked up their belongings and went along the street dancing in the dust, around, twisted into small knots breaking out running hard, their masks stuck close to the face. He saw on the ground the blinding snow fake a cheery robin, in the blue sky over his head a crow had stooped to kill. The lonely person following held the mask above the head, his own face shone out clear and bright. The actors in their dressing rooms had washed off the paint. He sharpened his scissors to cut out paper figures that posed and postured in the mirror and from the windows of the paper houses came the sound of shots, a bright eye gleamed and kicked up the dust.

Turn around and run baby.

Gun fire at the slightest provocation, he heard the voice and took his time walking home whistling for his dog waving his hands up towards the sky.

As he sat down on his bed his mother came in, at the mirror put on her lipstick. Turning around she picked a shirt off a chair and hung it in his closet.

Are you ready? She paused at the door to look at his hot face and speak about the dog.

He's around.

He waited until she had reached the bottom of the stairs before going to wash his red face. Out the window the field was still pink from the afterglow. The moon was hidden behind the house but the dog on the lawn had a bone gnawing it under his paws. The boy tapped on the window, it raised its head looked back over his shoulder, picking the bone up.

Happy?

Of course.

She took a breath, a deep audible one.

Inhale deeply. It's good for you.

He breathed sucking in all the night flowers, the leaves, small gnats, the slugs crawling on the damp earth, the turning smells of rotting leaves and blew them in her face. They slid past and disappeared behind. Her face shone out as before.

Let's be silent and listen. One hears such interesting things at night.

The wind rustled the tops of the trees and the dog lay down beside them quiet.

I thought we would hear the owl, we heard it the last time.

Hiding in the silence, losing its shadow in the dark, moving from branch to branch clearing its throat, it cleaned its feathers and waited. The bright eyes turned and watched to see the other animals of the night. The cold airs rose up from the forest floor, chilling the bases of the trees, cooling the thick moss. A large moth rested and fanned its wings, the soft edges bent and wrinkled.

The light had gone on and come up in the palace streamed

out the windows lighting up the foliage. They got up as she led the way and walked in the tall grass.

Close to the house, they peered in the darkness squeezing past the bushes that sat low along the side, looking in at the bright lights, the couples on the other side of the glass. The clock was sounding every quarter. From the hall a broad stairway led up to the second story, the dark corridors gave off the numerous bedrooms.

She went from one window to another. I can't see very well.

You're making too much noise.

Mrs Sterne smiled over her shoulder, passed by a laurel bush uttering little cries as her stockings ran and pushed up to the window.

Pitter patter, little feet ran along the carpeted corridor looking in all the keyholes and listening at the doors. Busy busy carrying step ladders here and there, up and down.

And if surprised?

Oh, I'm just pruning roses, sir. They do look too long. Won't you steady the ladder and hand me the shears? There by your feet.

The master is in his bedroom, the cook has gone outdoors and I am just for the moment the daughter in this house. Stop and talk awhile, hold my feet there by your hand, the rung is more slippery than I thought. There don't you think that's nice and perhaps we should take off this branch too.

Oh dear, I suppose I should have worn gloves.

The blood dripped from her finger.

Those thorns are sharp.

She put it out to be licked. He took her hand and holding it up to his face, pulled out the thorn.

Aren't you gentle and kind. Nature can be so cruel, but then these roses are such pretty ones.

She laughed gaily and taking the ruffles of her white dress in her hand she waved them around leaned into the rose bush and smelled a certain flower.

But the light began to fade, the moon was shrinking up, the clouds condensed around it, obscuring the surface blowing along tapering into thin points as they dissolved in the sky. The little breezes had stopped, the landscape was cool, the night noises had ceased.

It's been such a pretty night, she said and wrapped her fur close around her tickling her cheek with its long hairs, folding it under her chin.

The others walked behind, carrying the baskets, their heads lowered following in her path, watching her heels and the shredded stockings that hung around her shoes. They swayed with the grass, disturbed by her motion snapping back and forth swept in her wake.

In his room, where the moon had set and the window was dark, the boy rowed in the sky taking long strokes, leaning down to look in the water putting a finger out to test the temperature, to feel the texture and he tumbled after. The surface closed over his head, the cold precipitated under his skin. The owl outside opened up his beak and cried out in the darkness.

CHAPTER II

Dahlias, for the living room.

Yes, Ma'am.

Mrs Sterne held up the flowers in her hand wrapped in a transparent paper, untied the red string and took up a pair of toothed scissors to cut them to the proper length. The thick stems fell into the sink banging on the metal surface, splashing in the left over pools of water. She filled a vase and where the large bubbles writhed at the bottom put a green wire mesh to hold the ends. The vase reached the rim of the sink slipped in her fingers and exploded in the trough. Turning drops of water spun out along with the glass.

That's how it is.

The woman behind rocked up sucking in the sound. Her tongue released from the back licked at the succulent fruits, the sweet words left uncovered on the sideboard, creeping in the sudden silence to the corner she listened at a crack and dusted in the drawer. The afternoon in the garden she chewed on the grass, the hairs from the roots grew back on her hands to feel in the dark. The fickle hearts came in her spare time, they opened up and something new was sewed in, written on the flapping valve she found another name and at the end of the day walked down the road swinging her arms, bulky soul, to talk in the kitchen next door.

There was her face in the morning, again at night, and he was in the house or walking on the street. Her merry smile would find the way, the flowers bloomed and a wrinkle disappeared. Humming a tune at breakfast she kissed her husband on the cheek ate an extra piece of toast and when he'd left turned out with a new coat. That night she gathered her strength and shot across the table a bolt of poisoned steel. There, she said, I've had enough of you. He crumbled the crackers and dropped them to the floor, a nail banged deep into his thumb. The face was set in stone, he screamed across the table filled his mouth with venom and spat it in her eyes. They sat in silence while she finished off the meal.

I'll fix that Mrs Sterne.

Another vase was filled, she shook out the flowers with a snap of the wrist ruffling the petals smoothing the white velvet and turned each head to bloom in a different direction. They were carried through the house to the piano.

The clock in the hall struck eleven, Mrs Sterne stopped and wound up the weights. A bird banged against the window by the chair, fell to the ground stunned. There was a mark on the glass smudged feathers, her thoughts sank out of reach. It stumbled on the grass as she approached and took to wing. Annoyed, she thought. Crystal clear, sharp moments on which she liked to cut her teeth and the living room instead was sunny. In the corner the sun had burnt a hole on the arm of a chair, smoke spurted up and vanished, the edges of the hole enlarged crinkled and fell off brown against the white stuffing. She sat down, putting her little finger in the hole, turned it around and removed the burnt edges.

Warmed by the sun she took up her book to read, her body browned on the beach. Watching the days go by dressed in white with flowing sleeves she dipped her feet in the water, picked up the pretty shells and smiled at the fishermen. They danced in the night, they danced in the day, she tickled their beards with her brightly painted toes, and taking the light up from off the beach pumped it out into their eyes fusing forever her image on the back wall. Floating by waiting just out of reach and when she thought they might be tired flung her arms around their necks and sucked out an eye for her busy mouth. They called her name and no other, they sang her songs as the waves washed up on the shore, she ate the grapes, the humors pouting down her throat. The jets of jelly stained her white silk blouse.

In the hall the clock struck again, she stretched her arms the white dress flew up in the wind, the sand fell from her body, she opened up her mouth and swallowed down the flowers. The white and sunny room, the delicate pieces of china shone out, fragile, brittle balloons covered by blue cracks pulsing with blood ready to break bleed and stain the yellow rugs. She took up the tiny room so accurate in all its parts, each object placed with care and crushed it between her hands, the vessels burst in blue drops the light had gone, standing up faint on her feet she shattered the wall, breaking off the legs of every chair ground them into dust as they spun and cracked in her hands. Blowing the dust off the surface she looked around for more.

The flowers on the piano shone out their light once again straight to the pain in the back of her eyes picking out what she thought had gone, brightening them up so that they held in the breeze wafting in the window, gay opened up and unfolding their peculiar delicacies filling the room in the reflected light. She cleared her throat stroking the arm of the chair enlarging the hole smiled politely and left the room.

Turning at the door she looked back to the box. Rooted in position the tones were soft and whispered she should have broken them earlier while they were small, manageable decorations made for children with pink cheeks and long golden ringlets. The bell-like tones rang in the house on a summer's day bursting in and out. Mother, what shall I do next? Play nicely, dear. Carefully neat she curtsied before all the guests. Upstairs the houses sat on the nursery floor, she hesitated before the small cotton bodies, the tiny furniture, they swelled to adult size unbreakable fixed into place according to the latest style. The endless yellow plains of wheat painted on the wall had been broken by the rain and wind, the grain that littered the ground had been carried away in the fresh torrents that rushed down the hills. The shadow on the wall by her hand moved in the sunlight and disappeared when a cloud went by. She stood in the hall to go out, and took the car.

The water stretched ahead, at her side the swans turned their necks curling their heads down to the surface. The flowers in her hat moved in the warm airs stirred up by her passage. She leaned down and touched the children, their wings and bows, pink cheeked and chubby, they splashed and kicked, the men were on the shore dressed for the occasion in gaudy colors. Under the glare of so many lights, she showed her body arching her back rubbing her legs her thighs and up above the stomach round and round until she sank beneath the water, letting it flow in through her mouth and through every pore until the dissolution complete, she lay on the bottom spreading out her trap opening up the hidden places. The current washed at the filmy stems of vegetation green and translucent, the snails crawled on the cloudy sides of the tank scraping off the slime clearing away the dirt so that those on the outside could look in and see the curious body that lay within. Her muscles moved and writhed turning up the ponderous body, the eyes swelled through the thick glass and she died just then in ugly venom, withering on the floor. The heat boiled away, the moisture rising in clouds of steam. The blotting paper soaked up the blood and was wrung out, the paper fibers disgorged the burden but not the stain. On the swollen river crest her waves churned and tossed the battered bodies from rock to rock pushed along buoyed up by their decay, she saw their clothes floating on the oil scum.

The colors changed from blue to grey, the houses turned their shutters in to block out whatever light there was, to reflect it back on the blinding pavements across the street. The lights changed from red to green, the shopkeepers hung up their mirrors to turn the image around and with their backs to the light watched within the scene below.

She stopped at a red light to see a youth leaning against a post dangling his hands. She nodded her head parted her painted lips, straightened out her front and blew an imaginary kiss. Staring with unconcern he chewed his gum and spat on the road. It sizzled as it hit fried and gone, he did it once again his head sideways to watch with one eye the flattened world in one plane close to his face, the spot on the road. He put his hands in his back pockets and spun around. I know the likes of you. I'd pull it out and break it off. He dried up her false waters burning them on the pavement, spitting out to watch the vapors rise and form into clouds building and billowing in the wind. Lying on his back he watched the sky, the sun plunged into shadow by the dark mist. Thundering it would lose its substance to the earth below. Washed clean in distilled water, the turning surfaces on the green felt rolled and cracked against each other, he emptied the balls from the pockets and turned to see her car heading into another orbit.

She blocked him out and looked for other eyes in a different light. Finding a smile that didn't fade she raised her hand in greeting filled her cup with warm liquids which she proffered with a smile.

For a cold day when the feet grow numb.

He blew on his red hands to warm them up stamping up and down. Such nice flowers in your hat. I wouldn't want to see them wilt or change with the season. A cold day. Just to warm the tips of my fingers and the insides.

She smiled nicely distracted, looked into a store window to arrange her hat, to see the flowers, to see the man behind her looking over her shoulder.

Hello, dear, she said. She turned back in the window to

catch his smile and sidled out from under. Her hand touched her hair, perhaps another day.

Another day, he bowed. With his hands on his hips he stooped over, his head vibrated with the thrust of the blood from his heart.

She went down the block and turned to wave before going in the door, he'd left and she saw only the empty street brightly lit by the sun, the cold airs risen up and gone away. She walked inside on stiff legs, barking commands, sat down in front of the mirror, and smiled at the lovely cast of the head, brought her hand up to her cheek and smoothed out a lonely wrinkle.

Like this? The man behind cupped his hands around her neck and tilted it shifting the hair under his fingers.

She lengthened the back of her neck, chattered gaily on, shuffling in her lap the pages of a magazine. In the mirror the image continued, watched itself, twisted serious, not too short she said. Between the face and the surface of the mirror she unfolded a cartoon and sketched a simple figure. Mrs White, she began and drew the line from the mouth to the balloon filling in the sentences adding to herself and then out loud, last week. She squeezed it through and condensed it marched along in the square space the ladies hopped through their paces and stumbled over her outstretched foot. The husband walked behind she put in a firm stroke, rubbed it out not quite as tall and worried about the rain. He closed the door, cutting off the draft never very strong. Pinching her lips together she pried open the eyelid above her head, stopped the rolling eye, softening collapsing the hard surface pumped it back to full size, brightened up the glass and focused it in the mirror to look into her eye and smile.

Yes, that's right. With a pin she reached up and forced her way down his ear to loosen up the wax to open a passage to let the waves of her voice penetrate in. That's better now, her voice rose, there's so little time, she repeated. Her animate friends ran faster to top speed she went in and out of the market pushing her cart picking up the goods from the shelf. She wrote her own brand name around the package and the husband at the top of the stairs was yelling down the steps, hands on her hips she thrust them forward, arrogant little bitch that one.

On the street a car horn sounded she changed the position of her legs and taking all the strips of paper and film in her hands she tore them into little pieces ripping through the surprised faces, letting her fabrications blow away in the hot air of the dryers.

Turning away from the mirror she watched the other faces preening, repainting the silver backings of the mirrors to change what they saw within.

I'm in a hurry, it's too slow.

Gripping the sides of the chair she scraped down the nerves until only the single strands remained, vibrating high notes that set off the other threads tuned too tight. The air in the room, in the cubicles shook up and down, drew together and hit the same note. The intensity climbed until she blocked it out with her hands on her ears. Opened she turned her eyes, it had broken up and each voice took on its own tone.

How nice you look. How nice to see you. I must be dry. She removed her head from the dryer and pulled at the netting swathed around her head.

Dry?

Dried out, the luxuriant flowers wilted away, the proliferating damp places had sat under the sun too long and only a few edges of evil smelling water and left-over salts remained, few plants put up succulent heads in the spring, some broke out their petals in the night when the world cooled down and covered the round with a dry cold that kept the animals shivering in their burrows, the stars shone forth too clear, there was no vapor in the sky the white petals were hidden from all but the moth that knew the heart and took it before the first light when the petal fell to the ground and disintegrated. A hare bounded twisting and turning kicking up clouds of dust, he heard the shot as the animal fell and beat the ground with its furry feet. A small cluster of houses along the road were dilapidated and bare, a few chickens picked at the sand, the storm clouds up in the mountains at the end of the plain, they hardly came out and ventured over the flat land.

It would blow that afternoon. Ahead the clouds of yellow smoke rolled on the horizon. A dry wind is all that would come from the mountains.

He held the animal up, the ears fell away from the body, with his leathery finger he indicated the silky hairs that surrounded the opening into the fragile structure.

Soft and silky to lie on, those ears filled with hairs that welcome the sounds. A woman came and lay down crying her piteous cries that drifted and stuck on the long hairs, crawled down their length into the head. She would relax, the man nodded his head listening and lured her on. The hairs were stiffened until they pricked the skin and drew forth the unwilling blood.

23

Turned slowly to wax, the body melted in the heat and as he tilted his head the refuse drained out and dripped on the floor. He called for the girl to it clean it up and moved to another client.

She can go home now.

She looked in the mirror and straightened something. That's quite good this time. Snapping her steel rod shut, she braced up all the weak points and walked out.

On the street, she hesitated, paused in the hot sun and looked into a store window. She powdered her nose, another figure appeared small in the glass, approached busy flustered, took her hand held it and talked.

I'm so disturbed, she whispered, you've heard?

She had heard.

Mrs Simon, as Stella would say, had done herself in. She'd put it out of her mind. Her eyes went back to the window to look through the glass. Mrs Simon, she said out loud.

Mrs Simon, the voice repeated. The face was confused. You're so calm, she murmured. Who could imagine it there all alone doing it alone and three children left behind. Such a quiet person, who, would have thought.

Mrs Sterne let her eyes close, delicious sun, turning her head toward the sky she saw a lovely orange yellow.

Perhaps there was another man?

They say not. So thin, I'd never thought she had the strength. Her husband didn't understand. She was so kind, so thin like the wind, and always so vague.

Mrs Sterne's excitement fluttered and going one step further the drowsy sleep that took her away fascinated the pale

24

woman slipping to the floor with her eyes closed. So pretty.

In the window were curtains decorated with sunflowers. They went in to look.

Rather nice, gay and big. The colors, yellow and brown, striking and bold splashed on a white background. She saw them as they ripened, they were hanging over at the top and cut off, just before they were full, falling into a pool of water below. The seeds detached from the head and lined the bottom of the pool like pebbles until the decomposition was complete.

One of the children opened the door and found her there dead on the bathroom floor.

That's right.

The sales lady had brought out a sample of roses.

That's the wrong color. A little large and perhaps a bit ugly besides. She put her hand on the material and watched the crowd. Excuse me, dear, I have another appointment.

The wind blew papers along the street. She let the leaves drift along the ground red in their fall colors. When they stopped and settled down she walked over them hurried along. Stopped and looked in a window at an unfamiliar face, turned away. There's no one there. Unperturbed. And quite attracted darted back to look to fold it in. She placed the dress in the box and closed the cover, tied up and sent away. Playing hide and seek. Those that are mine, smoothed her dress waved and said hello.

Bubbled with smiles, on show and as she said so often, never frightened.

Her head was full with no holes.

❧ ❧

CHAPTER III

Pink transparent leaves floated over the bathtub, stuck to the rugs and to the side of the sink. On the stage dispersed among the pots of flowers a crowd of people stood, chattered and waited. Below a woman lay on the floor, against the wall were rows of geraniums, over her body the sunflowers dipped their swollen heads. Rolling over on her back she burst a sac of blood and spread it out on the boards. Mrs Simon smiled up at the faces and closed her eyes. The sun came through the window, its yellow shafts striking the wall and the white ceiling. The voices stopped, the scene was still, the painted faces looked down, the crowd broke up and drifted about.

The children gripped the strong stems of the flowers twisted and wrung them in their hands asking her what she had done. They turned her body over to let it drain dry over the roots of the plants.

We must do what we can.

Behind them a stage hand lit a cigarette and leaned back against the wall. The company came together the crowded faces shouting, the hall filled with the sound and a merry song, the rafters shook and bent above their heads high up in the darkness. They turned from their noise to kiss their neighbors on the mouth. The spiders descending from the ceiling were plucked from their silken threads to frighten the children who stood at their feet looking up at the reddened cheeks and noses squeezing out the moisture from their tiny handkerchiefs. Just at their level beside the knee they made a face and stuck out their tongues until the two damp unfamiliar surfaces met. A small child lay down and cried, a dog licked its face howling, she was pulled away and dragged through the crowd, the man held in his other hand his balloons tossing gently above the heads.

Five cents, have your pick, have them all.

At the side behind the curtain jars of pickled eggs and straight from the human body a fetus, they peered through the cloudy liquid, lines of people waited to look.

Mrs Simon unseen got up and walked away pushing through the crowd to the dark corridors, the doors were closed with cracks of light, she went out into the alley and the noise faded behind her. Black clouds of mist swirled around the street lamps, the dampness descended and cut across her face beading her eyelashes and her hair.

Her children came, their eyes wet, and clung to her knees, their lips were cold, they ran through the house bringing her boxes filled with what they had found. The long stems of the flowers were twisted and bruised tied up with rubberbands, she took a shell in her hand ran her finger along the ridges out to the point and put it in her drawer.

She walked outside the house and sat beside the fishpond, dangling her hand in the water, beckoning to the fish and stroking the snails that walked on the sides. Dried off she sat in a chair and turned the pages of a book, little flames burned up inside, flamed upwards and she ran and clasped the flowers that grew in the garden. Yellow iris, clear and yellow. Pots of them sitting in stores with steamed windows. She went in and asked the price.

Very cheap, Ma'am, very cheap. You like iris? Very nice. You want to buy Ma'am? Very cheap. Very nice.

Despondent, Mrs Simon went out. Her husband came and took her by the arm, leading her towards their home. The rain came and wet her feet, she stumbled and looked in the windows of the flower shops at the pots of yellow iris. Her husband went into a shop and bought a bunch.

You want something else, Mister? These roses is nice. Very cheap, very nice.

Here, dear aren't these pretty?

The woman filled the doorway peering out into the rain. Very cheap, she said.

They wave in the wet fields of the spring, the light rain filtering down onto their yellow crinkled edges. She leaned down to smell and the wind that came over the hill rustled the wet leaves next to her ear. The clouds rose up from in back of the hill straight into the sky.

Nice flowers aren't they, he said and she looked down at his feet that rested on the ground. They grew and took root, the gnarled joints bursting open with age and fatigue.

Aren't you too young to be doing that, she said, looking into his face. She reached up a hand touched it felt the bark and put her hand into a crack. Not much sap, she added, not that anyone would have noticed.

Her large eyes teared, they said she had married too early, thin and lovely. Vague.

She opened up his eye and looked into the black hole. Through the transparent stuff were long branching strands rooted toward the back. She followed them in, more and more opaque it ended abruptly. There was nothing left but the reflection of her face. Her dress creased and wrinkled she let go of his eyelid, pulling it down to shut out the view and joined the guests among the wedding presents placed on long wooden tables covered with white cloths rippling in the breeze. She ran her finger over the surfaces of silver and enamel and touched the materials of the dresses, which passed, pushing by. They stopped and shook hands, she smiled and said that she was very pleased. Thank you, you are so kind.

Her mother took her hand and led her away from the crowd into the house. She pulled down the shades and left the room. Below the sounds of the party continued, the sun beat through the yellow shade, a warmth crept across from the window towards the bed bringing with it the light and laughter, flecks of foam which coated her face and stung her eyes. She bathed them rubbing the washcloth against them again and again clearing them out so that she could open a book and read to pass the time away.

The shade hung against the window, a large bubble in the hot glass cast a shadow which grew and shrank as the shade moved out and back in the draft. She looked out of the bubble through the distorted glass, in the curve was the blue sky and below the lawn the tables the crowd. From without her miniature body was warped, the legs spread to the side, the arms outstretched pressed against the top, a large mouth and enormous thumbs eclipsed the rest. She laughed and struggled, beating against the glass, too small for those around to hear. The heat seared, the air already changing its composition. She held her breath until her lungs began to heave against the vacuum when her eyes closed she let out what was left, the bubble broke and she fell out.

The white flowers held her up.

I told you you would get your feet wet. Leave them alone.

Mrs Simon leaned forward and pulled at a stem. It resisted, her hand slipped and she sat down on the wet moss.

What did you expect?

The water soaked up through her dress, her husband turned and walked away. He never liked these expeditions of hers. She squeezed the water out of her skirt and went back to the road. It began to rain again, she held an umbrella up over her head and walked along, the colors of the late afternoon had faded, only the reds and violets were left shining out in the darkness. The sand on the road stuck to her wet shoes.

He leaned over the lawn on Sunday afternoon combing the grass, turning each blade parallel to every other. His hand on his hip he stared at the clouds. Just like a cauliflower, he said. Amusing.

Cooked and browned at the edges, dyed pink around the outside, she looked the other way, the wind was blowing hard in the distance, the tips of the trees thrashed under the force.

He asked for the clippers next. They trimmed the box into the shape of a peacock, its stiff branch tall stuck straight up.

31

Around the corner, just see what we put around the corner. The party of guests wound around the corner following the paved path and came upon the proud bird.

Isn't that clever, and a large button for the eye. Sewed on I suppose.

She thought about her plot in the country, a tiny grave covered with wild flowers.

He had said his word already. Covered with wild flowers until the farmer next door forgot and plowed it up, the bones cracking and breaking under the sharp edge of the blade. His dominant statue plunged forward, angry wrinkles on the face and he liked to walk arm in arm taking advantage of the sunny weather.

A guest, did she know him, was lying on the grass, his hands folded over his stomach staring up into the sky. The tray of after-dinner coffee came by. He took the small cup and knocked the spoon into the grass. Oh no, it's quite clean. He patted the lawn. Looking up he saw her eye. Mrs Simon won't you come?

She looked at his hand on the green lawn and shook her head. During the week she went to the museum alone, in the rooms machines hummed near the ceiling changing the air, a little orange light on an emergency box glowed in the shadow. She glanced at a painting, at a beach, almost deserted, there was a cold clear light, the clouds were high and thin blocking out the sun. A pail lay on its side near the water, just out of reach of the grey waves which broke on the beach. Two women huddled in their deck chairs absorbing the last filtered rays of the sun.

A little cold and a little late to try for the sun, don't you think? Always that and nothing more. I'd try the warmth and color somewhere else ladies. Not serious at all, just gossips. She pursed her lips.

The sand was caught on the small drops of salt water which remained on the skin from the last dip. The yellow leaves of the fall were in the air, she saw to the side a few children playing, too young to go to school. The two women giggled, rocking back and forth in their deck chairs. She waited until they finally retired in the cold to their bathhouse and withdrew her face.

The sun went down behind the hill, the rivers of tears moved with great speed the large running waves breaking over at the crest. Tossing intact, bouncing along, the varnish steady and strong in the salt she could see the bending fluid canvases, the rippling bodies. Her own eye floated too freely in the liquid, the light struck unevenly, the images were blurred and out of focus. Crisp and clear she whirled in her own wind, turning away the landscape flew up in the light. On the threshold between the canvas and the air the storm was far away. The thunder rumbled once and the woods fell silent.

She walked home with the change of season in the early evening of winter under the dark skies, the street lights were on, the store windows lit up, in the country were fields of blue snow and the lights shone far away, the summer sunshine would burn it away.

A door slammed on the other side of the house, she excused herself and passed along outside where clouds of leaves rushed by in the wind, leaves of carefully pressed plastic, she caught one and held it between her fingers, the crisp dryness of the drought had disappeared, the rubbery leaf bent, the ribs melted into the harsh green tissue. The moss at her feet glinted with moisture she put down a finger to touch the drops, the tough coating softened with her body heat and took the print of her finger.

The men were moving trees, a fallen bush was strengthened with sandbags, they added one more rose and sat down to paste on the thorns. The electricians carried cables across the lawn, putting up the night lights. She stumbled over the lines, her children came out to play ball knocking it up too high, she heard the sound of breaking glass, the workmen cursed and the game continued, they hadn't seen the broken glass under their feet. She thought she saw the jagged pieces cutting in, the drops of blood, but the bare feet stayed white flashing as before.

That's better, a voice spoke and a child startled, stumbled against the ladder. The workman dropped his box of tools tipped getting his balance spat at the child starting to cry.

She sat down on the grass and held its head in her lap. It looked up into her face with huge eyes, big brown and perfectly clear glass balls that collected the light. Moving forward further and further carried by the streaming rays that rushed in she fell into the brown material. The space between them had gone, the blue atmosphere turned to white, her eyes had been taken in. One round object fitted easily and quickly into the other, she looked inward at the small brain, she swivelled around to look out with sight of the child. She couldn't tell what the child saw. Her own face had gone. The background blurred.

The child blinked, whimpered and struggled to get down.

She let go, it ran hard off in a straight line, leaning to one side as if it would move in a circle but the straight line continued.

Grateful aren't they, an electrician was standing beside her coiling a cable in his hand. He asked her how many children she had.

Three.

The child disappeared into the woods on the far aide of the field. There and then not there. Cut out suddenly.

Mrs Simon sat rigid. The man offered her a cigarette. She shook her head, he lit his own and flicked the match onto the grass. Across the field she saw a round object come over the tops of the grass towards them. It bounced and strained, pulling at the string that held it down, gathered speed until it arrived in front of her. The small face was serious, unchanged in its expression, held with its eyes opened too wide. She reached forward to alter its state, but it withdrew from her moving hand, closed its lips blowing its cheeks out and then the rest of its head, taking in through the nose quantities of air with which to fill the empty spaces. She let her hand fall back to her side, the child stood there, pumping its chest, pushing the excess air upwards.

The electrician had finished coiling his cable. Nice to talk to you Ma'am. He walked off.

The child bobbed up and down, she walked across the lawn to where a machine was taking up batches of green tissue. The man operating the machine yelled at her over the noise.

It works pretty well, look at that.

The flat green sheets that were issued out broke up in

leaves. He shifted the levers and gears and they changed shape.

Have you seen my husband?

Over there.

Pressed out a thousand times. Accurate detail.

I think I lost one of the children.

The noise of the machine was particularly loud and hammering. A wind blew across the field and she could only faintly hear the men shouting at each other. She saw her husband leaning into the wind and dust, his chin jutting forward.

Gathering up her skirts she sat down and leaned back in the sun. The strong solution in her veins and arteries precipitated out on the top of a wall, her face was too big for the rest, her shortened legs barely carried the weight of her thickened body. The little people below looked up, she watched their eyes, held them steady plucking from against the stone the strawberries hot and sweet from the sun. A red flush appeared around her ears and the sides of her nose as she ate the berry. The vector currents carried the seeds to the cheeks just under the surface where they dimpled the skin and grew their hairs out into the air. With one hand she clutched a breast and with the other her skirts, smiled and the sensation spread out through the air, occupying more space than it should have.

Those who walked through the woods that hung their lovely leaves in complicated patterns, with such softness drank in the sunshine respiring gently letting in the air through the pores and holes, dying with such startling colors in the fall, would stumble occasionally on her petrified face. It protruded up from the earth surrounded by trees that lifted themselves

36

into the sky, their longitudinal tubes strung in concentric circles. A hardened face with stone lips that were cracked at the edges for the lack of proper food.

Pretty, isn't it, a little touch of nature in the room, especially in the evening when the fire crackles at the side flickering on the pleasant faces. She rolled to the ground heavy in the back, engorged all around vaporized with the smell of the strawberry, the hot sun close to the earth and to the stone wall. The clouds came and dimmed the light.

She went towards the house before the storm, the clouds rolling in and rain was falling in a field not far away. The dry wind rattled through the dead sheaths of grass, whined in the telephone wires and lowered the temperature.

The house was dark with the approaching blackness, she lit the lights and climbed the stairs.

Her son lay on the bed turning the pages of a book. She sat down beside him as he flipped through the pictures and she ran through the paths that hung with rose bushes, thorns and high grass. There was still some damp remaining from a former rain or night dew and her feet were wet.

Stop and look, she said.

He reached in with her words and took out the trees and flowers dropping them in her lap. They fell and cracked, the tears running down her face blurred the remains. She would take the colors, the lines in her hand to put them together again, in a flat surface of textures to hang on the wall. There, she would say, the flower was back in paint, the breeze that she couldn't see fluttered the petals. Her child reached up to touch the salt tears and her cheek. She saw his face far away, his lips moving.

It's going to rain, shall I go out?

If you like.

He snapped the book shut and ran from the room.

The black clouds came and sat over the house. She went to the window but the storm was going to pass over. A line of blue slowly widened, the wind came up in fits and died out altogether.

The child looked up from the lawn disappointed.

It didn't rain.

No, she said, and retreated into the room, it didn't. She heard the thunder far off.

Mother.

She went back to the window.

You can come out now. The face was horizontally held just below, the cheeks red. The head went back to the up and down position after a few seconds. That makes my neck hurt. Does it yours?

The blue streak grew, the sunshine approached. The child lay on his back exercising his stiff neck.

She went back into the room. It is too bad that it didn't rain.

The sun flooded the floor, the last cloud had gone, she could feel the heat pouring in around the feet of the chairs under the bed as far as it could reach. She heard the running footsteps of the child following the line between the light and the cloud. The air in the room turned and rolled, heavy and humid, it lapped against her feet, drew the blood from her head until it emptied out and could be carried with ease.

I don't understand, she said.

She walked back towards the others, another student was waved up to take her place.

I'm not feeling very well.

I should think not, the teacher replied, turning her back to watch the blackboard that was crowded with figures.

Mrs Simon took up her books from her desk. The room was quiet, she looked in turn at each face and each face faded away, they were writing rapidly. She opened the door and slipped out.

In the mirror the expression was fixed and staring, a woolly stuffing poked out through the holes. Taking a tweezers she pulled at one of the strands, then changed her mind and thrust it back in. It could laugh but then it wouldn't stop. Gusts of air rushed out, her eyes widened, the voice was small and she couldn't hear it very well. She tried to close the mouth pinching the lips together and pushing at the jaws, the eyes slipped beneath her fingers rolling and she couldn't get a grip on the eyelids. She slapped its cheeks to try and make it talk. Exhausted, to get away she plunged into the garden running wildly catching at the plants, the sky, the warm smells. Stopped by a blue flower, a bee landed, hovered, landed. She got down with her face very close. A small child came near and put out a finger to touch it.

I've never seen that before.

The child leaned over and took the creature in its hands, left, running down the road blue skies behind, blue skies in her hand, changing in the background all polished up for the day.

A smooth china head, too round, slipped through her fingers

and fell shattered on the ground. The fluid ran in all directions, the ground which was parched and thirsty sucked it quickly up with bubbly sounds of satisfaction. She picked up the broken pieces, avoiding the sharper edges put them in her purse and walked along the road. The aisle of trees led the way she saw the light at the far end and hurried forward.

Straight into her face, down the alley the insect braked in front of her legs spread wide pushing against the air, the belly was extended pumping, the hairs bristling as it blocked the light close in. It exploded backward as she wiped her eyes the light cleared, the parts were dissected out and much enlarged. All there for her to see, to trace with her finger, drawn on a chart. An even step accuracy at all costs. She entered the room, closed the door smartly. The students would be instantly quiet. Straightened up tall she unrolled the chart and pinned it on the wall. There it all was, the intestines in three dimensions, the mouth parts, the eyes in cross section, muscles spiracles antennae drawn and labeled and to go with it interesting habits of a particular species, the life of the bee she thought. Her head was light and well organized, the students smiled and talked she coughed discreetly. They told a joke and she drew the structure of an insect hormone on the blackboard. They picked up their pencils to write down the effects. Is there anyone here, she began a student leaned over a microscope looking at the little stiff body, dried and preserved, the light was reflected off one of the wings, it flashed in her eyes abruptly she rolled up the chart and left the room.

She found an empty road, tapped the drawing on the fence posts as she passed raising clouds of dust that rolled around her head. Her brain stained black as it penetrated inside. Confused, she thought. Cross sections of that wouldn't be useful, the landmarks would be hard to see and the microscopic picture useless. Black clouds in watercolor, flattened and stamped. The hot muggy day, unrelieved, was beginning to have an effect. She sat down beside the road, the disembodied forms reassembled, joined up flew into the fields to taste the flowers. Nice combinations of colors and muscles against the blue sky. All put back in place again, she opened her purse and dumped out the shattered head. Picking up the various pieces she tried to fit them together, but the edges stubbornly refused.

She knew the man who could do the job, he put all the pieces in a pile of sand standing them up and with infinite patience did the work. His whitened fingers had lost their fat, she snapped the tendons, tick tick against the bone, the finished product was of hard baked clay, she could see that it was old, he didn't need to say but she took his free hand.

Talking he could reconstruct the conditions: atmosphere, the percentage of the various elements, the source of energy, and then with the proper charge the system would spring to life. Any system. In the cold winter the long shadows vibrated on the walls in the light of the fire. His hand drew in the wet clay charred black in the fire, filled with a liquid that jelled in the cold, the stories that were told, he repeated, are always the same. He stood up, and opened the glass case, take for example in stone. I could hear his voice with just a little effort talking in my ear. She saw the light coming in through the window onto the dusty shelves, the door must have been left open a crack

41

but they were cleared out long ago. She had just been acting old fashioned. Flouncing her skirts she pushed her hand back towards the light towards the winter, pushed and fell. The heat of the flames burst up inside rushed out to the sky and pulled forward in tears the flowers and shapes of clouds walked over her small body crumpled in the dust.

Oh yes, she said. Her clothes were damp and she could see that the man was distracted by the appearance of a wet spot on the floor.

That doesn't fit into your plan of attack does it? she said.

He shook his head.

She kicked it over, put it into a different perspective and walked in. Her feet stepped along on top of the lines that led towards the back, towards the center point where they all converged. If they bent with her weight that was another problem which she wasn't going to worry about they could deal with that some other day. If the children played skip rope and engendered strange things in the landscape that was because they were young and didn't know any better. She proceeded by herself into the projection spun away in the wind losing her balance and fled into the holes in the ground. Little by little when she thought no one was looking she came back, her mouth in a lilac bush, her leg from the knot of a tree and her eye in a stone. A nose came to smell the blossoms, she sat down on a twisted chair and laughed.

The lilacs were cut from their stem, she reached for the hand that held them, stretched in vain. Games, she said,

They're not yours, he said a little angry, not projected out of your head.

She was sad, the tears showed in her eyes. I know that.

Try again.

Her finger tips touched the surface of the flowers, the color came off, she could see it spreading out over the surface of the sea picked up in the waves, blown by the wind whipped into spray which got into her eyes.

The dusty roads led between the high banks of grass, the blue skies and clouds were in front of her. She could hear the sounds of the farm machines in the fields above her head, the steady chug chug of the baler and the men talking. Walking until she no longer heard the sounds, she climbed up the bank holding onto the grass pulling herself up until she stood in the field. The men lay sleeping their heads encrusted to the ground. She sat in the grass and waited, relaxed in the warmth of the noonday sun. The cows stood to one side, their backs dappled by the sun shining through the trees. The men would never raise their heads swollen in sleep, the leaves that she had seen moving the light were still. The suction was strong pulling her dress, legs and arms, she let go and was taken away. The smiles were gone, the tears, the black clouds, she leaned down in her speed and picked all the flowers she wanted, the yellow petals brushed her cheeks. The warm air blew rustling the grass. The sleep that rose out of the ground came up through her body and drove out the hidden beams of light. They washed against the solid surface of the sky and glinted on the cut plane of a blue stone carried on the finger of a hand that rested immobile in its colors on the arm of a chair.

X

Chapter IV

There had been a storm during the night, the rain came in through the partly opened window, spreading puddles on the floor that trapped the bottoms of the curtains, saturated them with water and held them anchored, wet and heavy against the breeze. The trees outside were still dripping, the sky broken and running in the wind. Patches of grey blue spread in the speed of the change, the hidden sun just rising, brightening the borders of the clouds. On the floor the water was beginning to evaporate, leaving concentric lines of whitened wax and precipitated dust. Pink powder fluffed up by the night wind from boxes on the dressing table dusted the room, floated on top of the liquid forming a scum, a sodden powder puff trailed its long hairs in the water.

Mrs Sterne held up the bed clothes and examined the body that lay underneath reflecting the color of the blue sheets smelling warm and heavy. Moving the toes at the far end, she smoothed down the folded skin, pushing it towards the bottom from where it had risen in the night, from off the bones. A wet curtain came unstuck from the floor and flew out into the room spilling water onto the rug. She slid her legs out from under, stood up staightening her nightgown and shut the window.

Turning through the room by the mirror to the bath she

saw the morning face and ran the water, the air bright with steam, eased herself down inside and popped the soap bubbles with her long pointed nails. Her head turned working itself around, below the body swelled up absorbing the water and filled the tub, solidly packed and sat in the mold. It lay resting, brooding the jowls didn't move and the eyes were shut. Her hands caressed the warm skin, mumbling endearing words she stuck out her tongue flicked it and opened one cold eye to freeze and thicken the skin. She rumpled the toad-like hide to see the eggs beneath rolling under the pressure and squeezed one out through an aperture. It throbbed alongside a breast, rolled to the edge fell to the floor and broke. The tub moved with heaving gasps of laughter her body changed color from pink to red and she stood up with a loud noise as her body came unstuck from the enamel surface.

Standing in the middle of the floor turning in the vortex of the flame and the currents of water that fell towards the drain, she wrung herself out spun dry and wrapped her skin in a towel. The wrinkled undersurface was rubbed with salts, the outer dusts with powder and she stretched it over its form.

The lower rooms were beginning to warm with sun yellowed in the new light. On the lawn outside the robins were out for worms running in the wet grass and she drank her coffee in the kitchen. A fly was trapped in the fold of the curtain buzzing, the two women fell silent. She caught the fly between her fingers, the tiny squares of white cloth came together and she felt the insect quiver and crack.

More numerous after the rain, she said.

Stella brought out the fly paper and hung it from the over-head light.

The steam rose up from the sidewalk, coming up with the sun. Down the street her mother sat in her brown wicker chair next to the window bent over her hands feeling their texture waiting for the door to open.

She spoke immediately, I'm very old, Ethel, you should take better care of me.

The air in the room was crowded with dust suddenly visible falling to the floor.

I can hear those nice birds, what do you call them, running on the lawn?

Robins, it rained last night, Mother.

I know that dear, robins. I saw them as a child.

Their feet made noises on the grass and they came with a black eye while she lay on the lawn to sleep, to look between the fingers that she had spread out on the lawn. It smelled nice close to the roots and earth.

I can't smell anymore, did the doctors tell you that?

They did.

And what else?

You know as much as I do.

Nothing as far as I could see.

For heaven's sake. She sat down on a chair.

Her mother wrapped herself up spun around with tiny threads attached to a leaf to be eaten at some later date. Winter insects were found sitting in the corner cold and stiff, left there unable to find their way out of the house closed for the winter.

The windows were nailed shut, the shutters locked to keep out the wind, rain, and vandals. On the floor the line of a shadow shifted, the caretaker would come and draw back the heavy curtains hung against the cold, they swung along the rods and the darkness in the room was gone. The muscles that had been lulled to sleep in disuse and the damp cold broke out and turned her head.

My dear Ethel, you can't imagine the dirt and the dust. They had to use a broom to move it first, the vacuum cleaner filled up too quickly. Like on the moon, or didn't you know that there is dust on the moon. Or perhaps there isn't.

The old woman saw the spring sun come through the window thawing out the bones, waving one foot and then another, they peered with bleary eyes into the world stretching a wing out along a leg. The tired sap frozen in the bodies rose, pumped up by the tiny muscles. Her temples burst with pain and heat, the light came back through the haze of the winter night. Bright gleaming spots, her flowers growing up from the ground, a day when she was warmed in the light all the year round, the insects never drowsed and the dogs laughed in the garden as they buried their bones again and again. Her laughter spun and rolled, the curtains blew through the windows the grass was green and above the sky was clear and pale blue. The streets were quiet and the fruits in the garden ripened fattening in the sun, the surface hot while the cells inside swelled in pride. The water ran through wetting the roots, the owl called at night and woke those who wished to sleep, the angry man came to the window and looked out into the soft night

47

with a large moon. He chewed his cud and lay back down. From inside the immobile spots of intense color bloomed with perfect form into brilliant flowers of blue. The naked center of the bud drove out the darkness into the morning sun.

Iris, she said, they turned out to be. Sprinkled every day to make them flourish. Very young an early love, they sat together in the bath staring at their eyes until the feet that held the tub off the floor took wing into the sky. She laughed and loved and said a dozen things, somebody came in the night, sawed off the legs and it sat immovable, flat on the ground. Nothing to do but fill it it with flowers and vines that would creep over the side.

The short bursts of bloom, the days she remembered had recoiled away coming back sometimes with a sudden swiftness planing on the swell and wave of her memory and overwhelmed she was ground down into the sand losing her breath. The flowers in the garden went to sterile seed, those inside spots broke out into proliferating growths tainted with blue. No more brilliant petals soft and fluttered by the wind. You wouldn't understand would you, Ethel. That makes me very happy.

In case we might cry in each other's arms pouring the tears forth and flooding together in some sort of sentimental horror, two rivers draining out at their mouths into the salt ocean.

The old woman shifted her position in her chair, with a trembling hand pulled the rug a little higher in her lap. The movement raised the dust that lay on the floor and she saw in the garden those rusty legs and claws. The covering had come off in the rain and the wind which scooped up the sand and blasted it across the empty wastes. The rust crept in from the cracks and the open wound made by the saw, it ate out the rotting nerves, tendons and bones that showed at the end of the stump.

The more primitive growths the multiplying cells swept through the body stuck on a rough spot, she walked by a bush covered with white flowers that grew in the corner of the yard. The heavy smell charged the air and she sat down on the curb of the road. A band played down the street, she waved her arms in time to the music and counted the buttons on the front of her dress. Ten. Was that all they wanted to know? Sensitive cells, the doctors said, her memory no longer benign. The arm swung back on the record player and the piece was played over again. Her doctor laughed, when she was alone her hands touched the bandaged head and she felt the tears run down her face.

Her daughter waited in the silence standing on the beach, and heard the voices of the children playing in the water. Too loud, she turned and a swing rose too high, a young child screamed with fear. There was no need to worry. She looked over the sea wall, the rats ran on their long legs across the sea-weed cast up by the last storm whipping their hairless tails. The salt water was a brown green washing with short sighs over the rocks and pebbles. Never let babies lie in the sun so pretty and pink. The blood red face shrieked with each outgoing breath, the steady rhythm beat in her head, the arteries and veins stood out of the neck, the feet were beating the ground, rigid the sunstruck brain was covered over easily by the sand that was carried in the wind to fill up the holes and erase the blemishes. Stuffed eggs, they took out the inside and put it back in again, her teeth gritted on the sand. Sand papered cheeks.

She moved the old woman into the wheel chair, arranged the rugs and rolled her out into the clearing air.

Her mother was whispering, gently gently, the ears were swinging, the eyes hanging on the ends of long cords: pendulums. They hit on the edges, the sharp corners brought out the blood, she shook out a handkerchief mopping it up. Singing, swinging on the outside air. Planing on the swells, maddened by the buzz of a bee that had flown out of its nest early in the morning, exercising its wings, testing the air and packing in the pollen.

The wheel chair ran along the sidewalk, she looked straight over the head of her mother well above the sounds that issued forth from below.

The playground won't be too noisy?

I don't hear anyway and the old woman gestured in its direction. The children ran in circles, the swings moved busily back and forth, the nurses pushing them higher and higher at the strident urging of the child. The slides were crowded, the mothers sat knitting around the outside. The wheel chair was surrounded by a whirl of running children.

Careful, let the old lady alone.

Mrs Sterne caught a child by the arm, her nails dug into the material of the coat. It pulled away in fury, ripping from her grasp standing still its lips clamped together, the chin wrinkling beneath. She lowered her hand to hold her skirt and turned away. The child quivered set out a high note of closely packed waves, the heat boiled up in clouds of steam, the system exploded and condensed in the cold on the dust in the air to drops of water that splashed on the pavement. He broke away running to the other side throwing out his arms, leaning forward his head touched the ground burrowed in and he flipped over and over banging down as each separate spin began. The nurse at the other end put her hand to his head stopped the progressions and sat him on the bench. The other children were still wrapped in their heedless circles.

She pushed the wheel chair away.

A child came up and stood between the knees of her mother looking with wide open eyes into the wrinkled face. It reached up its hand to touch the side of the mouth, the lips twisted shook and searched sideways for the finger to suck its flavor.

Dazzled in the sun the grandmother waited in the field, she'd pulled out her chair while she sat a hare leapt from its hiding place and bounded away, the hunters walked through, their feet muddy from the summer rains, and as they went the edge of the horizon rose up in a circle. As the sun's rays fell behind the lines of trees overhead they started to climb the increased slope with a deliberate slackened pace. The hare reappeared to try another path, fell over its feet and rolled down the incline to the bottom where it rested panting. The light came back as the sun rose with the continuation of the day.

She grasped the fingers of the small child in her hands, in her convex mirror the tiny world arranged itself, the sea lay quiet at the foot of the cliffs, the animals beneath opened their flowery mouths into the sea. A dog yawned, his back stretched lost in the muscular effort snapped back in the blazing sun into the heat. A plane far overhead passed the tiny circle that opened out onto the sky, under the rafters of the house, a wasp papered its nest and a beetle slipped in the loose sand that formed the sides of a funnel and fell to the spider waiting in the hole, its front legs extended and ready.

Slowly at first and then rapidly inside out, the force of the movement throwing off the ground into solid light, the grass had gone, the men, the animals, peeled off pulverized, material no longer, her own thoughts had turned out like all the rest, gone and imposed on the sky.

She took the head of the little boy in her hands and squeezed gently. A little pressure and the canals widened out until all the parts were spread evenly on the surface. Exposed to the light and air devoid at last of information her head had gone before its time, the bubbles rose to the surface warmed in the depths near the center the heat was lost to the outside and the memories brought up floated away forever unperceived. The green leaf wavered on the twig, jerked a last time and fell away, there were little round holes where the insects had taken nourishment, holes through which you could see the sky and the clouds.

She turned her head so that the boy could see the profile. Can you see them?

He touched her head. It's all there.

Clever boy. The evening and the stars faded in through the twilight, she leaned out and cried in their presence as the shadows blackened the ground, the next day at noon outside in the fields she heard the sounds of the insects high in the trees singing as their jaws worked through the green materials, the holes had spread further than she thought.

They look so undernourished, Ethel, those children. Innocent little things playing on the jungle gym. She snapped her fingers. It doesn't take longer than that. The bone splits open, the inside peels off, comes out, looked at, seen and gone.

She stretched out her hand to the child and held it towards him until he took his own out of his pocket and shook hands with her.

Good bye.

All finished?

All finished.

He clicked his heels, pivoted and marched to the opening of the playground swinging his arms and hands up shoulder level, a soldier of the king.

That's enough or we will lose him altogether.

The cold winds blew over the tops of the hill, picking up the dead leaves in their force, blowing them forward up into the sky where they spun in circles to drop back in the calm that followed, drawn back by the suction to the fields and woods, into the park through the iron work, the black rods that extended themselves to the sky. On cold winter days when the park was empty each person ventured out leaned against the wind pulled his overcoat around and shifted his feet to keep them warm. A casual visitor picked up a stick and waved it in the air, the squirrels snuffled the cold leaves and the pigeons were lined up on the branches of the dead trees. The man stood, the ducks under his glance squatted closer to the ice swinging their tails. A whistle blew from the sea, the grey clouds moved swiftly overhead, the red color of his scarf faded in the dark.

Cold in the winter, a man passed.

The visitor leaned back. Looks that way.

Lays the dust though, in the summer the light hardly comes through.

A squirrel was turning endless somersaults. He stopped to pick up a stone and tossed. The stone rattled in the branches near the animal and it stopped.

Got to break the circuit occasionally.

The squirrel sat gripping the branch tense and stiff. It stared at the two men.

Uncomfortable that.

The man was spreading seed on the grass. You think so? Bring your children often?

They like the playground.

Speak to the old woman?

Doesn't everybody?

I used to see her in the old days before they put her in a wheel chair sitting in her car in the shopping center parking lot beckoning to the guardian. She would smile and wave her hands until he came over and then she laughed and laughed locked inside her car, knocking on the windows carrying on, the poor man didn't know what to do next. She would press her face to the glass flatten her nose, he could do nothing but tap on the windows to try and make her stop. When he went away to get help, she prettied herself up stepped out and in perfect order went into the store.

The other man rubbed his hands, blew on them and put them in his pockets. She talks a lot now.

That's right, mister, she talks now. They say it is malignant.

They listened to the sounds coming from the playground brought by the wind.

Chatters takes you by the hand fixes your eyes and talks, stops people on the street and children while they play on the long winter days when the black branches of the trees stand out against the sky and the noise from the playground drifts across the grass. She stretches forth her hands, gathers in what she can remember from the air around her, while her daughter sits by her side rocking a carriage slapping any face that falls into tears tightening her wrinkled stockings shrugging her tiny shoulders and smiling apologetically at those who come too near.

The black clouds of the afternoon crowded around, the crow that sat in the top of the tree softly tried his voice, snapping his beak and hoisting the wings higher up on his back. They crossed and recrossed at the top settling in, dropping back to the sides as he nodded off to sleep. Dingy blackbirds with red eyes cut their toes snapping off the ends with their sharp beaks. Drops of rain came in with the wind spattering on the grass. Waiting until tomorrow the two faces bent over their game shuffling the cards and dealing out the hands.

The wind tumbled the apples from the trees, they rolled on the ground into the gutters and onto the road, the thin wheels cut through to the juice, the woman pushed the apparatus, the wheel chair came close on its way home.

I always liked to see the animals, the squirrels on the ground. Push me closer, Ethel. For the children on Sunday afternoon. To put their fingers in the fur. Careful dear it bites. You don't have to tell me about Mrs Simon. I have heard.

Roll me along faster, so I can hear the wind blowing through my hair. There are my friends, do you think they remembered what I said? Would you like to get home?

Her daughter raised her head even higher, above the storm and the clouds. Her nose twitched in the cold she saw her mother from many miles away running shriveled on the ground falling on the grains of dirt. She was pulled up into the sky by the wind, the skull swelled and burst on the road. A mess on tile floor, she looked and left it to be cleaned up by someone else. Her mother rustled beneath her, shifting the blankets, giggling.

Is it so very funny?

Poor Ethel, left out in the dark, caged out with the children in dirty clothes and with big heads to burrow under your skirts. There are my friends holding hands.

She laughed and pushed the wheel chair along. There's no reason to stay here, Mother. You'll only get cold.

So many things to see, the color of the sky, the clouds. Weren't those people nice? I've seen that man before out on trips, Ethel, what do you suppose he does? Walking around at this time of day watching, everyone. Some sort of voyeur, I suppose. That's the way some people are, filling up the empty spaces by walking in the park. Others do it for you. Touching isn't it Ethel.

They left through the gate of the park and ran along the

sidewalk. The old woman hung her head and let it swing. Crack crack. Ethel picked it up and rested it squarely on the neck. Gone for the day, not until tomorrow. She wheeled it along, her mother woke as the chair bumped into the house. The eyes teared and dripped.

Did you notice? No make up so it won't smudge.

The blankets were unwrapped and she was moved into her chair faced out toward the window.

Just go along, Ethel. There won't be a puddle.

><del>¬</del>¬<del>¬</del>×

Chapter V

One two three, one two three. She accentuated the one.
One two three.

A finger missed a note. Shut up. His face was red.

He waited in the silence, she paused.

Don't you dare speak to me that way.

I can.

Such an infinite fuss for a little boy. Just keep right on playing. I wouldn't dream of saying anything more. She shut the
door, her steps receded on the other side.

One two three, hop hop. Jumping along on one foot he came
down with each step flat on the pavement, his body shuddered,
the toys that had filled him up that morning were jarred up rising
into his mouth, the taste stung in the back of his nose. He spat
them out, the cloth skin broke and ripped on the pavement, out
came the stuffing. Lightened up and skipping, he floated down
the road, all the way through and out the other side.

His grandmother was sitting with her back to the door facing
out the window.

Your mother took me for a run in the wind. Blew my hair
straight out, pin it up boy pin it up.

It's all right.

Have you been to the park.

No.

I'll take you.

She liked the ducks, to put her hands around the tightly packed feathers that coated the body. Strangely small and thick, they looked so cold standing on the ice, their wet eyes poking out from the skin fixed and unmoving.

The head moves, Grandma.

Screws up tight, she said.

The boy clicked his tongue, sat down crossing his legs. She turned the chair away from the window, wiping her eyes with her handkerchief.

And the robins, she said vaguely, on the lawn after the rain.

Taking the hem of her skirt he pulled it to wake her up, she took his hand. The white skin of her leg was transparent, the large veins twisted up on the outside. He ran his finger down the length pressing out the blood. The vein was emptied and stayed flat, he released his finger and it filled up from the bottom. Repeating the operation, he looked up at her face.

Leave it alone.

He got up and walked to the window.

The rain has dried off?

He nodded.

Does it smell?

Can't you get it?

Stuffed up too tight, she said and pointed to her forehead. My growth.

Does it hurt?

Not often.

Like a headache?

In the sun. But even that goes right through, she smiled, to the back of the neck. She put her hand on the spot. They turn into such pretty colors. Have you seen?

In the shade of the tree the tiny breaks in the foliage let through the sun projecting circles on the ground. Such a bright sun that bears down on the tightly mowed greens. She took a pliable stick and flicked it with a terrific force, the head following behind the billowing wand. Crack, she watched the ball disappear, and reappear bouncing along the fairway. Run down and watch it, boy.

My guardian, she said pointing out the small figure to her husband.

He grunted. Make a fool out of him if you don't watch out.

And who's making a fool out of whom?

My dear, I wouldn't worry about it if I were you. He'll get there by himself.

She was angry, crumpling the handkerchief in her fingers.

You should be nicer to your grandfather.

He's not here anymore, Grandma.

To his memory then, her face was small and tight. He died of the same thing. Only it was localized in a different spot. She dropped her handkerchief. He picked it up and she saw it fall into ashes pulverized. Flicking her stick again she moved the ball along the fairway towards the green. Behind the grass turned to black and the clouds came up in dark rows. She spun around to see her husband in black and white just taking a stroke. He stood and watched the ball go, leaning on the club.

Come before it rains, she said, hurry up.

He looked and put the driver back in the bag.

Hold it, she snapped a picture and waved.

She put it on the shelf and when the days grew dark she ran her finger along the cellophane surface, caressing the grass and when he was in her plane of vision they stepped together out of the house, her arm in his. The old people black coated trembled in the cold on the front steps and sat down on the bench to watch the passers-by.

The tears came, she had sat and waited too long watching a flower come up in the spring. She leaned down and touched its petal, sat back and waited and they both were there when the night came and the moon rose in the sky. It closed up with the first breath of the cold night air and she came in out of the damp. It had wilted the next day.

You have to press them, Grandma, under books, dried you put them on large pieces of paper with their name.

She ironed them flat and removed all the wrinkles.

Glass flowers on the table, soft blue iris with a streak of yellow running up the petal. Fresh flowers always in the room, spring for every morning. My friend. She held out her hands to her grandson. My friend, I'm so glad to see you. Your eyes are so bright and gay. Her own rolled up. My friend.

Her hands touched his and he drew away, her fingers tightened and held the tips of one hand, the eyes came back and fixed his own. Forgotten already?

He rubbed her legs with the palms of his hands hard. Warmer?

Much warmer, she smiled, like rabbits. I had them as a child, that kicked, white with pink eyes and a toad that hummed underneath the skin, eventually the humming stopped and that's that. A sudden silence and all the noises you liked so much are gone.

He hesitated looking at the ground, the dusty road where the carcass lay.

In the faraway blue, the clouds moved along the edge, the crows flew just under the horizon. There, there's a flower on the ground, pick it up and place it near the tired body. The smell as it escaped would scent the air, and take away the smell of liquefaction. Put it in the sun and dry it out. She sat by the side of the road to wait for the night before leaving.

He looked out the window, the rain had begun to come down, she was walking down her road leaving behind the flattened dusty shape, speaking to those people she met, waving her hand, dancing swinging her black skirts. His lips straightened into a thin line, a long thread which he pulled out with both hands, tightening the knot twisting the frayed ends between the tips of his fingers.

Snapped the string, opened out his lips hissing whistling through them and just where do you think that came from, Mrs James? He tapped her skull with his small fingers, the words that came out lined up one by one on his belt. Opening up the mouth he peered into the dark caverns, lit them up with his light. The room melted along the crack on the ceiling, the walls fell away, the outside air cold came in around his ears, his grandmother small he twined his hands in her hair pulling at the white strands pulling then forward around her face tying them in a knot under her chin.

That's the way it should be. And how do you suppose that those noises and notes came to be the way they are? A bow around your neck, a seat in the other chair, propped up with one more cushion, a bowl of warm water for the feet to circulate the juices underneath the skull and beneath the skin.

He peeled it all off to see what was underneath, layer by layer until he thought he was down to the very center, down to the navel. He took the kernel in his hand and placing it in a tube of water watched the bubblings the changing colors. She floated to the surface, he pushed her underneath and she popped back up.

And now, he said, and now. Folded in the words caught her small body and held it tight, motionless in the air. She was talking again, another day, another chance.

From the ceiling the old spider webs hung broken off, below his feet was the weave in the rug, a pattern disengaged. The light that came in through the window stretched out, the line of the window bar lay across it. The dust in the light moved slightly, the threads from above swayed in the currents in the room and he moved his hand watching the shadow.

His grandmother continued, she was listing the people who had been at her wedding. Mrs Green, she said in a loud voice, Mrs Green came in a white hat.

He lifted the carapace of the spider off to see what was inside. A confused tangle of grey. He squatted down pulling out the white thread, his eyebrows raised, it came out sticky and lay on the floor.

Mrs Crane with her husband in the third row, not that I really thought too much of her, but she might as well come to be nice.

He clenched his fist and the knuckles turned white.

And who knows what they thought, all those eyes lined up in the pews.

Is it just because you are old, Grandma?

I am as they say very lucid, child. Your mother has been telling you tales.

Have you seen my hand. He put up his fist and pointed to the whitened knuckles.

Pretty little thing.

And under the skin?

The skin was stretched tightly over her forehead, the bone directly underneath. Within, the smells and perfumes had overwhelmed the countryside stuffing the air, the white flowers multiplied their petals, the leaves had choked the ground and weighed down the trees. The tough weeds hung on flowering in the mist from the spring that hung in the valleys rising from the floor of the woods, working with the clock around the day, the sun had been out and burnt through to the roots of the grass and into the thickets of the forest. Tic tac the hands slowed down for the afternoon and hesitated on the edge of a small flower that sat low in the grass, just out almost hidden by the overgrowth. She touched it straightened up and ran like mad in the afternoon tearing through the fields, the hands spun around and what could she do but stop and watch. Her breathing had choked in the heavy air.

Outside into the sunshine to the cheering crowds. Shake their hands. He went to the window and drew a line in the dust.

Smiling talking, here boy come and hold my hand.

He put out his hand and touched the dried out skin, whitened until it had a tinge of yellow, the blue color of the curtain was reflected there, a bit of green outside came in parading on the floor as well as on the skin. Her voice echoed in his head talking, quietly calling his name when he wasn't listening playing with his friends on the street, he held his breath.

And when you were my age, he looked at the yellow photograph on the table, and just before.

Bounce bounce, he played with his ball, rolled it on the floor.

Happy, eh, Grandma? He took her hand, shook it solemnly, all smiles and gay.

Her grip tightened around his fingers and let go.

Chapter VI

The boy had left playing outside down the street, the noises were faint, the grandmother turned her chair back to the window and looked out at the lawn. The birds she had noticed before were gone, flown over the wall. The breeze in tips of the grass had left them still, the folds and wrinkles on her face froze, only the eyes turned in their sockets, in the back of the room the shadows were black in the corners and close to the floor. Her face held out toward the light she put her hand against a vessel in the neck to feel the pulse, her ears reached forward to pick up the sounds, she pulled them to the chest the noise boomed with a wash of blood coming behind. Laughing loudly to fill the room to shift the curtains she bubbled over frothing wiping the tears from her eyes, no change, she settled back.

The sun was out. How bright the colors are. A blue sky backed her up, the fresh colors of the new leaves approached in the clear air.

Her friends had come to see her walking up the path pointing at the flowers in the garden and the red tulips beside the door.

What a lovely day it is and the lawn looks so well.

She poured the tea and dropped in each cup a slice of

lemon. The sun was out behind her head shining down on the back of her neck. She leaned forward to pass the plate of cookies. Pleasant, she thought. Had they been on a trip? Perhaps they would introduce her to their friend. She saw their island with a brightened eye.

The husband spoke at last, are you waiting for someone? Would you like us to go?

She had so many things to do and the maid was coming that afternoon.

They got up to leave, they liked her flowers, those large red tulips.

She settled back and let the sun come down. It would warm her up and thaw her out. How nice that the garden appeared in such pretty colors for her guests.

The rain drenched clouds tore away and were dispersed by the wind. She snapped her fingers, the heat rose from her toes past the knees and further, in the excitement she saw the curtains sway in the breeze, turning and turning, the window was open and the summer airs were coming through.

The lonely voice started to sing, the notes came out slowly on the warm air towards the window out from the shadows at her back, the tears were in her eyes the thickness of the water distorted her view, the drops catching the sun and her voice filled the silence.

The minutes passed and drowned out the sound, the notes she knew disappeared was it her guests who had forgotten something? She turned around to look toward the door. The shadows had moved to her head, they darkened her vision from behind a dark wash poured down over the surface until the contours vanished and she felt the light that came in the window changing its intensity and turning away.

I must be very old, she said. Her hands reached forward to push out the curtains of black, they met no resistance and she put them back on the arms of the chair. The door swung in the draft, she went outside, out of the dark carrying her black hat and coat over her arm to the church. A few minutes rest to say good bye, to join the others who had come off the street, they would hear the service, and she could be alone again.

The dark figures crowded forward dancing on their hands, the gravel of the roadway sticking to their palms. She closed her eyes as they flipped with the stronger music, the discreet organ had filled the background, and tasted their lips that split open to grin. A silly face kissed her mouth, sang sweet words into her ear empty and had no weight floating helter skelter in the air. She reached up a hand to pull them down and listen.

Sweet lady, caress your lips and hold them tight, lightly sew them up and give them up, blowing gently all the while. Come hold my hand and dance. Cackling loudly talking of the things they think they have done.

With parrot hats, the green feathers led down the sides under the chin, hold your ears they repeat and repeat, again and again. Unsatisfied she reached back to play it once more, those voices babbled on coming in from the past, drawing herself up cold and distant, those others would die around her. She changed her mind filled the heart kissed her daughter's hand and gave a quiet smile. It's all done once, but for the second time. She smelled the flowers and rolled on the grass, I could have played it another way and who would you love? Led to her chair with her hand on her brain she could feel the lumps even from without. The wrinkled tired petals drooped by the side of the bed, pumped up and refreshed inside her head, they dropped again when she turned her eye. What's she done and who could help the tear, she asked. The words from yesterday floated through on the tops of the waves enveloped in foam pushed by the wind broken in the turbulence of the toppling pile of water, falling as the bottom slowed down on the sand.

The water spread through the room, and she floated on the crest of the wave singing again her voice drowned out, unheard.

Would the time never pass? Her fingers lay useless, opened up, the shadows had opened their mouths her slow eyes extending their tongues to take up the dust on the floor. She giggled behind her hand, would someone see her if she laughed too loud? She'd walk boldly out the door and say good bye.

I'm just going out for a moment. She leaned over the figure in the bed kissed the face and walked out into the corridor.

He's just the same, she said to the nurse, no change and she came every day walking up the steps and into the long corridors.

Shall we put flowers on the grave? Before it's done? Or should I wait? Real flowers.

She walked among the grave stones and looked at the plastic flowers. Are you sure that's right, she asked. They don't wilt.

The thought is permanently there.

Or permanently absent as the case may be.

A dead thought, she said pompously. Week after week with no sign of wilting.

She cast a real flower, wrinkled in the afternoon sun. The petals dried off bloomed to their full color, a red rose too bright perhaps in the white room.

Shall I cover them up, she asked, is it too much?

The weight of her blossom bent the stem toward the table.

She blew into the ear that lay exposed on the sheet. The warm air from her mouth rushed through his head, the eyes changed the line of direction and she saw in the shadows the dust move in the eddies. The changing shafts of light billowed in the corner, a face come out from the clouds. White and fluffy, bright with hope, she had always thought that the storm can only clear the sky.

She tried a laugh to hook up to the inside, her brain would smile. The links were broken, the facial contortions brought no relief. She pulled at her lips to show her teeth. A smile that comes and goes, that flickers at the corners. The corners of a child on the run, on the run backwards.

His stomach had given him trouble, all covered over with a perfectly good skin that hid everything very nicely.

Are you also getting old, she asked. The nurse in her white uniform was bending over the bed. The voice of her daughter was coming down the hall.

Here you are, she whispered. Your father's about the same today. They stood while she twisted her white gloves.

There's nothing really you could say.

The nurse came in with another chair.

He's spoken to the night nurse but she can't understand.

She didn't stay very long as her mother had thought, with the issue no longer in doubt.

The grandmother turned away and cried, the white room was washed with tears, it held her tight she was taken out and taken home. I don't really care, she thought. That poor woman Mrs Simon down the street gone before her time, sad little thing she was, sniffling like a rabbit and poking that nose around with tired little cries. Couldn't take it any more, I suppose, crushed under the burden.

Need a little sun? Stella dusted in the back. She moved the wheel chair closer to the window. The roses are coming out on the trellis.

And when you go?

Mrs Bates, when I go there'll be no trouble, fast and easy.

The old woman laughed and cut her roses to put on the stone. Blue like the sea, ruffled in the wind, more sun and water to make you grow. I haven't enough gossip for you, she remarked. They've all gone over there, rotted out and pale. I cut those flowers every week and no one would know, they are so old they can't see anymore, it's too late, I never loved. Ha Ha and still alive. Their poor old eyes straining in the dark with nothing to see, or a glimmer once they turned their backs.

The garden was pushing up through the ground, the flowers appeared on the stems folding out after the leaves, she watched with interest and forgot her lunch.

❧

CHAPTER VII

It is such a heavenly day.

For a drive in the country.

They rolled along in an open car, past fields and farms.

How lucky it didn't rain today.

The women had put on their bandanas, the man wore his hat.

The car was moving very fast. They urged him to slow down.

Not scared? He laughed.

You should have let him bring the dog.

He doesn't mind.

They rolled along a little faster.

Perhaps we could stop soon.

I know just where I'm going.

At least there isn't much traffic.

They spun through the narrow roads bordered by long strands of yellow grass. The valleys opened up, past flat potato fields through the marshes and they stopped by the sea that rolled up in long swells, long flat swells that stretched in both directions as far as the eye could see, they came in small and broke just at the beach. Even on a windless day that raised no spray.

How nice there's no wind. No sand in our faces.

Or in the picnic.

And easy to bathe. The two women walked together.

The boy chased the gulls.

The man sat on the sand facing the sea, the baskets and rugs heaped up beside him. With a frown he watched his grandson, turning his head away from the women who walked arm in arm, their heads bent together. The boy took off his shoes and wet his feet.

Are there any fish?

Here? He sat with the incoming waves just reaching his toes. I don't see any. He looked out at the regular pattern. In the waves? Swiveling around he looked back at his grandfather sitting up on the beach. The eyes were held back in two hollows shaded from the sun.

Can you dig to the other side?

Nobody can.

Somebody might.

The sky was light blue and far away, no clouds. The gulls circled high over the water, the women walked through the sand whispering in the monotonous wash of the waves. The child had wandered away and called to the gulls who came down and sat bobbing up and down over the waves, ducking their heads the drops of water gliding over the waterproof feathers. A boat on the horizon moved out of sight.

Isn't it nice that the beach is empty today.

There are never too many people on a weekday.

It is lucky.

Yes.

And no wind.

Look at those little birds run, I can never remember the name.

We might rest here and sun. They lay down and uncovered their bodies, lying side by side their faces pointing up toward the sun.

Two plums lay in the open, their skin red and glossy, underneath the yellowish flesh was warm and offered no resistance.

You shouldn't eat before lunch.

They won't be back for a while, they are having a look at the sun.

He sat with his back very straight watching the sea. It broke through his head, rolling up into his eye and crashing on the back wall. His grandson played at his feet and the beach grass grew out of the sand through his head up to the sky and the clouds, touching the top of his skull the roots were in his toes. In the narrow furrows the women lay arranged among the stems. He raised himself up and walked into the water. The boy ran down the beach kicking his heels, the sandpipers flying before him out of the spray. His head as he came out of the water swayed in the sunlight, he spread his toes in the sand.

The women came and unpacked the lunch, handing out the sandwiches, uncorking the thermos bottles and they lay on the hot sand facing the sea, wiping away the wet salt.

He touched the hand of his wife, his face rolling like the sea. The steady swells were coming in at the same height holding the movement from a distant spot they couldn't see where the clouds lay in a hot circle and the sea turned around itself whirling off at the edge.

She came away touched and floated on the rim of the sun cutting off the rays of light, her body blocked them out. The black shadows of the clouds raced along the surface of the earth riding the hills and filling the valleys with a cold wind that would bring the rain. The edge moved fast speeded up on the slopes, in the wave she was carried beyond the shore. Surprised she lay out in the sun exposed, the boy was on his feet and down the beach, her daughter complained of the sand in her mouth and she vaporized in the heat and floated in the eye of her husband.

He saw her face and turned his head, she washed up against the side of the sphere gasping for breath. The boy held up a shell and the water dripped out. The dry pieces of sand jumped on the impact the spots darkened spread over the surface of the beach coming closer and closer until they overlapped. In the stillness came only the sound of the rain, the drops which hit the beach and fell in her hair. The sea was flattened but still rolling in, she stood in the downpour in the cold and cried out with her weak voice beating her hands against the sand which turned up white and dry from underneath.

Trapped in the eye and suddenly wet, she knocked out the side and let the sphere drain dry. The liquid rolled down the face. The sun dried it up, the salts were encrusted on the cheek. She regained her feet and ran away held back by his hand, the figure sat all alone up straight beside the picnic staring out to sea. He was calling the boy and watching her face, watching the sea roll in from the ocean and he called her name again and again.

They finished their picnic in the silence, they walked together hand in hand into the sea. The salt water held them up as they floated in the swells rising up and over the humps. Four heads bobbing in the hot day, rotating gently in the currents, their white skin came up through the water projected toward the surface wavering in the shifting planes of waves and ripples. Her head was down, the magnifications changed, she touched her toes moving her hands under the water feeling the bottom just below. Beyond the water's edge and beyond the white sand the beach roses appeared in the green, the red color faded pink by the sun and whitened by the sand, the fragile tissue ground up by the constant movement of the sea, washing up on the shore turning over the grains of sand.

They turned to look at the flat horizon and sky over their heads, he took his women by their tails swung them around flipping off the scales, scraping them off against the grain. The silvery plates accumulated on the table and on the floor until only a thin network remained covering the flesh beneath, a silver network that began at the toes and swept over the rest of the body ending in a knot at the top of the head which he attached to a hook on the wall. They swung gently rolling over their round surfaces, he leaned over and kissed their feet. Her eyes had watched, he held her hand and bowed over the water.

The boy by his side was filling up the wings of a large rubber duck, he took his hand and pulled him along through the foam.

Where are we going?

Up the beach.

That part was wilder, the beach rose and beach grass came closer to the water encroaching on the sand, the clouds were gathered over some inland hill. They climbed up on the shore and looked from the top of the dunes. The low bushes stretched away from the beach to the hills in the distance, open country like the sea. They steamed in the sun, the dense smell distilled into the air. The afternoon had been interrupted in the heat, the only sound came from the sea. The duck lay stranded on the shore its red body shining on the sand, the boy watched while his grandfather lay down in his blue bathing suit and went to sleep with his back up to the sun. He sat down beside him and counted the swells that came rolling In. A hawk turned over the dunes low over the grass, by his feet trailed a line of ants, his grandfather was breathing deeply into his arms.

Tic tic tic, he supplied the sound of the watch, they didn't have to see the shadows move, the smell grew thicker the sky rounded over his head and tied him in.

The other children had gone home, he would wait for someone to come. It won't be so long. The crowded mothers had looked his way they could start him in the right direction. He searched among their heads and talked beneath his breath. I could cross to the other side.

He could see out beyond in the wilderness and saw the stones drying up in the sun, withering until there was nothing left.

If you play nicely someone is sure to come. But they bickered among themselves. Give him a chance.

He thought perhaps they had small heads of flowers born

with those petals, pink like the beach rose and fragile. They were talking about someone else's child.

Around that corner would come her large hat with the red flowers, tossing waving through the bushes. He put in two dots for the eyes and colored in the very small white face. The neck was long and he stretched it out.

The head jumped on the line, sank in the sea and he reached over to wake the sleeping form sinking his finger between the silent ribs pulling on the skin that gave beneath his grip. The sun had taken away the scent which wandered down in the valley, the body was rooted to the ground and turned to the sky, dazzled by the white flesh he saw flowers at the mouth with their stems deep in the throat and their roots far down in the stomach curling and twisting. The sea came up around his legs and pulled him away, with his hands he broke off the flowers and held then up. Waited with the present in his hand, they stayed fresh and clean.

Fresh flowers, he called.

Beach roses could decorate the flat stomach. The shadows shifted on the sand as the sun moved in the sky, the flowers trembled in his hand. Given to people? The sound of the sea was monotonous, he pushed it down and it came in again. Sheets of hot air rippled up from the landscape, his small hot body cracked, the water wet the sands and the flowers lay tangled at his feet. He took up each one washed and dried holding them up to the sun to watch the light come through the tissues. If I should die before I wake, the image in his eye would leave no trace. His small head raged in flames, the sun falling lower shone in his eyes and his grandfather woke blinking and sat up.

The small boy smiled and looked away.

They walked slowly back through the sand, dragging the duck, the grandfather was silent and the boy held his hand. The women had bathed again and were drying their bodies.

I'll always be your boy, he called up from below.

Such a sweet thing to say. Where did your grandfather take you?

Up the beach. He went to sleep.

Did he turn red in the sun, like a beet?

The little boy laughed, and I ate him up just like that.

He lay on the sand and rolled over under their feet, into the sea taking the salt water into his nostrils and throat. His sides were ticklish, his skin trembled over his ribs, he rang the bell holding her hand. Wrapped in a towel they carried him up under the dunes with his shovel he filled a pail with sand, packed it in and turned out the pressed cake. The stems of the flowers were inserted, the legs of the women much reduced stuck in, the toes wiggled until the sand fell away and dissolved at his feet.

His mother sat down by herself, the breeze in the late afternoon was moving out away from the beach toward the sea, she wrapped herself against the draft and lifted her head to the sun for its last rays. The noise from the outside, the sound of the waves came beside her ear, she stared through the screen the waves were breaking in, the solid fronts cut up by the tiny squares. The sun grew larger as it approached the sea, she pushed against the wire strands that kept out the flies, her head appeared in each tiny space. The water was grey, pulling her towel around her shoulders she hurried forth, pushing open the screen door and letting it slam behind her, her sandals left sitting on the doorstep. The sand was still hot, distressed she ran picking up her feet as fast as possible carrying them toward the water. The breeze pushed the ripples out to sea and she reached for the line of the sky, too small and far away her arm shrunk back to her side. The fluids lapped at the border, the ocean came up towards her, the waves agitated and cold, she stepped back.

Changing guards and holding hands, cracking her bones and chasing a point that ran before her in the night just before her outstretched hands.

She said a few pleasant words to her mother sitting beside her, gathered in all the warmth left of the afternoon and held it inside her towel. In vain she thought as the sea turned from blue to grey and the shadows thrown by the uneasy movement of the waves were black. The light mist that formed obscured the horizon, her skin began to lose its color reflecting the color of the sea, loosened by the water she pulled it off. Clinging to the beach in her chosen spot her head rounded down and shrunk into the neck, she rolled with the pebbles, grating soft noises as the water washed between them rubbing off their sides smoothed and polished. The soft rain that fell sweetened the taste just at the water's edge.

She turned around to look, beach roses and beach grass, brightly colored umbrellas stuck in the sand, the yellow sand so close and so attractive, sprung up to talk. Each warm grain harbored in her mouth. Brightly painted people sat in rows facing the sun and sea and she welcomed them all by name.

It's only recently that I have come to know you, she remarked, that we have been introduced. That's a becoming suit.

Isn't the sea nice today, just the right temperature.

Sailboats pleasantly dotted the water.

My son adores to play with boats.

Tell me your name again? Perhaps I have a son that age.

We should leave, Ethel. It's getting cold.

They packed their things, gathering up the towels and the remains of the food and took one last look at the sea. The falling sun had grown large on the horizon, the dust and atmosphere changing its color from white to red. The sea had turned to red.

❧

CHAPTER VIII

In the late afternoon, the grandmother had put away the tea set and was sitting on the porch. A cloud formed behind the trees and she watched it come over the house. The evening shower would cool off the air, the flowers that had wilted in the strong sun of the midday would suck up the water and straighten out, their stems flattening and stiffening with the liquid. The whole bank would lift their heads toward the sky. The gentle rain came and put down the dust, cleaned and washed she lay down to sleep away the hours before darkness. In the monotonous sound of the rain she waited near her pillow until she fell with the pieces rounded out into drops. They fell and were shattered by the wind, splitting with the gusts into a finer and finer spray, the dampness spread into the house and down to the cellar. The fine moisture rose in the drafts suspended drifting sideways onto the leaves of the trees, onto the petals of flowers and inhaled into the lungs of those around her who strained to catch their breath.

That's my girl, she thought walking by herself in a long alley of trees by the sea. Always there on time, running. The surf was breaking on the rocks, the water smashed in the holes tossed up into a fine spray. The heavy breathing disturbed her sleep, the rib cages heaved and sucked, the mist turned in the tiny passages, rushed in and pushed out in the cold air she could see their breath, fine clouds. They let go and took in the same drops, words that they had spoken, delivered and then swallowed. She couldn't hear. The heavy sounds fell to the ground, spreading out like a thick smoke along the sand, reaching the waves swept up in the turn and the fold. Wasted away, the last breath gone she drove on alone. The ribs of clouds that turned and turned in the curvature of the sky held her attention and she watched to see the bars replaced by a slim cover of white film that would eventually thin out the sunlight spreading it out evenly. The shadows were dimmed and in the grey differences of shade the colors were bleached from the leaves by some solution, white like the stems she had seen in the woods living on a source underneath and curled over like pipes.

She bent over, the mouth opened and the pipe let go, water poured onto the ground from the straining face and ran away in rivulets carrying small grains of dirt colored muddy brown washing away the sweat she could feel accumulating on her skin.

The clouds overhead moved by, the flat fluffy oars that curved like ribs surrounded the compact body of a fish thrown up from the sea onto the sand. She put her hand around the scales and held it up, hanging on tight as it jumped in her fist. Its mouth opened and closed, the gills threw out their red filaments toward the air, gulping down the absent liquid.

On the beach the receding waves had left behind a corrugated surface. The pools of water were ruffled by the wind catching the light and reflecting the blue in the sky which she couldn't see. Holes that breathed covered the wet sand, tiny fish and shrimp fled with the wind and raced toward the open sea. She saw them on the outer shelf and then over the edge of the cliff falling out of reach of any light. The fish, placed in the sea, lay too weak, the waves turned it over and brought it back.

The long beach spread out in both directions as far as she could see, the ends were bent away and the sea curved down in front. Behind her back the crows came out from the dunes walking with the gulls on the sand. In her sleep the sphere shrank and dropped falling in the night from the sun toward the stars. Losing her footing falling over her feet, she splashed in the water turning from the laughter that came from behind and tangled in her hair. The nurse set her upright and held her arm, on the beach she moistened her hands where she could see the inside liquids cooling to the surface and bubbling over. Her feet were in the foam, the tiny bubbles burst on her skin at the tips of her toes, just under the nails, vesicles of perfume that held the smells of the sea, she popped the black sacs on the seaweed between her fingers.

On the dunes she picked a leaf with a gall. It was filled with dry shreds of cardboard, which drifted away dispersed by the breeze, sucking them back they stuck in the sections of her lung. She coughed and squeezed each sac from the bottom, the tiny sacs that collapsed and expanded, and forced the air past the tightened muscles. Her ears picked up the high-pitched sound the sighing of the wind as it passed in the trees pushing the leaves through the telephone wires and washed the tips of the grass in the meadow. The sand and dust blew into the air carried in the heat billowing towards the sky to the tops of the clouds coloring the sun in the sunset, the suspension scattered tne light until it came through in the evening, red. The watercolors ran on the paper, the water soaked into the fibers and dried away, the pigment left holding onto the threads, the pure color broke down into purple yellow and brown, the borders of the clouds were uneven, her wet brush spread the new colors too far and they merged into a uniform grey.

The foam bubbled in her head. A light froth lifted her thoughts away into the sky splattering on the side of the bone, expanding inside the thin film pushed until the pain she felt pervaded her fingers delivered to whatever she touched. Cysts, she thought, full, that might burst and flood the rest. She could feel it trickling down through the planes of tissue, a thick viscid material flowing in oily lines, a brimming bowl that promised some delicious cream dessert that would fill her mouth and remove for the moment the pain. She touched the sheet with indifference scooping out from the hollow surfaces of the head those bits she hadn't seen.

The sun on a hot summer's day beat into every corner, the oppressive heat was under every leaf, the shade more suffocating than the light. The colors of the flowers broke away from the background and came in the house. The insects were flying in the air, the buzz loud in her ears. A deadly green entered into the eye, the flowers opened up and held out their parts to be fertilized, the cells of the stems were moving the water up and down. On the back of her eyeball the sky reversed itself, the clouds bent on the curved screen floated from one side to the other.

With the extra growth of cells on the line between the eye

and the air uncontrolled the leaves were oversized the flowers multiplied their petals and the dampness was absorbed by the growing plants, the mist was dried away. She swelled with the water buzzed like the flies and followed a trail of ants through the grass into their teeming home where she was laid among the other eggs. Her evening walk had commenced her legs ran in every direction, the florist had sent flowers. She held the petals in her hand and crushed them to moisten the air seeding the eggs onto the rough surfaces into the cracks in the stone. They rooted in breaking down the rocks dissolving away the binding glues.

A disordered sky ran in her mind, the clouds built up and let forth their rain. The rose packed itself so tight with red slender tissue that it never opened, only suffocated and dropped off the stem. The stream was choked with water weeds, her feet walking along the bottom could no longer advance. She lost her balance and fell into the unfolding patches of green swimming with the goldfish trapped in the net.

Her breathing troubled her sleep, she woke in the middle of the night. The distant rumbling of a passing storm sounded outside the window. No one there at that time of night. She waited in the dark for the fresh breeze to take away the heaviness which held the bed sheet hot and sticky, a cool fresh breeze that came off the water at night blowing in from far away, from an empty sea.

She felt the curtains sway in the window, dimly she could see their forms move into the room, the wind came out from underneath, the flowers by her bedside trembled and were still.

The coolness came over the drops of moisture that covered her face. The curtains had moved again turning white, catching the outside glare from the stars and she cried in their continued billowing turning over the pillow touching the empty sheet and smoothing out the wrinkles. The curtains were held out just clearing the floor, she rested the night awake watching the light wind come off the water, listening to the sound of the night birds moving past her window. The soft breeze of summer touched the ripened grass, her eye poured out its greenery into the night. Before it had died in the heat, she moved out of the sun into the shade to lie down and rest. The morning came, the afternoon, the night would never end she stayed where she was lying in the thickly growing grass.

✦

CHAPTER IX

Mrs Sterne had a free day, the flowers were arranged and she circulated in the empty house through the rooms on tiptoe turning with the music resting on the night before, she stood upright and swayed into their faces, took the lapel of one particular man, put her nose into the button hole and talked.

I have only one son, and how many do you have?

He laughed in her face cleared his throat coughed and sipped his drink. Two sons and the wife dead. His lips mouthed some words she couldn't hear.

She looked in a mirror applied some lipstick to try some other man.

Just a flower he smells when he's unhappy. It's such a disgrace to drink so much.

They took away the drink, give her the flowers, there'll come a time when she'll be too old and there won't be any more trouble.

She put her head on the arm of the sofa and opened her mouth. The guests crowded around to feed her cherries, outside on the lawn the couples danced, she wandered on the grass in her stocking feet, hid behind the bushes waiting to rush out. Is there no one here who knows how to dance?

They took up her plaintive cry, there's no one here quite

like you. The orchestra played her song, she danced under the open sky. A man took her arm and drew her aside. Lean against my shoulder and she leaned into the grain of the wood. They danced between the trees and into the flowers. He held up his hand and brushed back her hair, black eyes and took the cherries held between her teeth. The night was passing and they turned to stone dropping one by one into the water splashing in the pools in the garden. The party lasted very late, there was no moon only the japanese lanterns that hung in the trees swaying in the breeze. The shadows of the leaves were very large on the ground.

She waved her arms enfolding pockets of light throwing them away into the shadows, into the water and walking up for more. She teased his eyebrows, cut a flower to put in his buttonhole and told him to flirt with someone else.

There's no one here like you, she said, putting her hand up to brush his cheek. Have you seen the lanterns by the pool? His chin was strong and firm. Hold my hand and take me for a walk. There are the reflections. She leant down and disturbed the surface of the water, the ripples spread out carrying the light with them. He held her back as she leaned over too far.

That will do, she called, there's only one way now. She held the cherries up above her head, their crimson shiny skin tightly packed. She burst out the stones and popped them in the ground. They found her a watering can, the long neck stuck out over the disturbed earth and the spray came forth lightly covering the spot under a mist of water. Puddles appeared and they cleaned off her satin shoes on the grass.

I hear you Mary Bell moving through the fields, cutting through the grass, the clouds are high on the horizon, flowing white carefully washed. In the fields below, the poppies grow among the stems of yellow grass. The child is there as you wade through the grass in your long gown and wide hat, running before picking the flowers, catching your skirts and jumping the streams that traverse the hill. The sky is light light blue, the sun bright white and casting a golden glow. Come with me in the afternoon, she brought her basket for the flowers and for the berries, her day under the bright sky and beyond the hedge, through the gate and into the field, holding up her skirts above the ground swaying over the lawn and down the path.

She dipped her pretty feet into the water, rinsed her toes, washed in the cracks. They are all so nice, she said, she gathered the flowers in her arms and smelled the fragrance, flowers for the living room. The white flowers looked cool in the heat and shone out in the night. He's my one and only savior, the rose bush on the lawn. There's a deep red color in his cheeks that spreads all over. Is there no other person whom you want to see? She raised the question and then let it drop, dropping things into the pool one by one. She liked to see them bigger on the bottom, her shoes that planed down, a jewel in the waves. Her giggle was picked up in a spray of water and showered out in little drops, silvery drops lit by the japanese lanterns. Flung them out along with a ring, a shimmering note. Bubbles and tear drops that changed their shape. She waved her fan, the air currents would buoy them up. Her lips pursed and blew, the ripples carried away the sound on the pool. Liquid notes she heard over the field, from the lark that hovered in the air above the fields of grass and poppies, the notes of joy and laughter that came to her ears in the morning through the open windows from the light blue sky.

The sounds would disappear into the ears that rested near her lips as she turned on the grass under the lanterns, her head lay on a cheek, reclined on a shoulder and spoke into an ear. Her lips touched the skin her hand tightened on the back, bare feet on the grass she spun with the music. Dearly beloved, she spoke in the night, my heart is with yours. The fragrant smell of the night blossoms came to her nose, the perfumed air held in the fold of her silks printed with patterns of black and white flowers.

The man talked about the owls in the tops of the trees. Feathers in your hair, he said pleasantly, stroking the back of her head.

They walked to the edge of the crowd where the lights gave out. Far away they could see the sea over the tops of the trees. Lights were moving near the shore.

Look, she said, look at that out there. She spread both her arms wide flung them behind her and gathered them back over her breasts with a sigh. The edge of the terrace dropped to a black shadow which swung out from the wall until it met the light moving out from behind them hitting the meadows that led in the direction of the sea. Moths flew over their heads heading in towards the brightly lit porch and windows of the house.

The lights of the sea, the voice spoke loudly in her ear. Those are the lights on the sea. Stars on the land twinkling in the haze. He put his teeth on the lobe of her ear, his tongue touched the warm soft fur, she sank to the ground under the sky looking out into the darkness towards the sea. Her dress was spread out onto the grass, the night dew came across her skin.

Come, she whispered.

The daylight was coming in the windows brightening up the wall. She turned off the light by her bedside and got up to look. The grass had been flattened by the dancing the night before, a man in an open shirt and black pants walked slowly around picking up the bits of paper and disconnecting the lanterns coiling up the cords. In the daytime the sea was barely visible in the haze of the summer heat rising off the meadows, the sky was partly overcast. A table for breakfast had been set out under the trees. A warm gust of air moved up the valley came over the wall and blew away the paper napkins.

In the hall the flowers her mother had gathered sat in the shadows, roses that had deepened their color until the red had turned to brown. The leaves were dark green and withered.

They should be thrown out.

Perhaps. Her mother had lost interest.

She had her first taste of coffee, patches of sunlight came onto the grass, wavering with the movement of the leaves, came closer and played in her hair shining through. The little spots of light worked inside, moved in her body. She felt the flapping wings of yellow butterflies in her hair, their feet touched her skull, they hung onto a moving petal of a flower, a waving piece of grass. They flew in and out of the head, the light danced in her eyes flickered through the foliage. She took her scissors, put her hand at the bottom of a tuft of grass and cut a poppy. The soft petals drooped and bounced. Flowers for the table, they won't last long, but the color is so pretty.

The heat was going to be oppressive, kept in by the clouds, even the wind was hot. The clouds so nicely washed had shadows on their bellies.

She lay on the bank when it had been warmed by the sun and smoothed the folds of her white dress.

She drank a glass of lemonade brought on a tray. The sun was hidden by the leaves of an oak that grew by the water, she moved her rug back into the sunshine and gathered the yellow flowers that grew on the borders. On the inside of her head the round spots of light played crossing and recrossing. The spotlights ran on the dark clouds at night, on the stone. Putting her hand down she felt the warm pavement, put her hand around the bunch of flowers and took them inside. She walked to the window, the morning was very long, the grass from the mower drifted in the air, the smell was in her nose. The flower she held in her hand thrust its middle into her eye, the yellow pollen was shaken loose flying away in long streams on the warm air.

Peeped around the corner, the sun flashed in her eyes, she withdrew to sip her coffee and tried once more to see. The landscape had opened out, spots of color appeared in the fields, the hot summer sun came through the clouds, she got up from the table and walked to the edge of the lawn.

So pretty in the early morning, so nice to look at. Mary Bell I hear you moving there, so lovely at this time of the day. No one else is up. She looked back at the house and waved her hand, put her foot forward into the tall grass, walked ahead into the meadow. Her skirts were carried high, they spun over the dewy edges of green, her legs were brown and tight below. Smiling faces had lined up on the path, she pursed her mouth touched each one gently on one corner and then on the other, lightly pecking. The edge of the lip was of a stiff material, she brushed across and talked on her way. A full moon round and big lay in the sky, she took a neck with her hand and bent the head down carefully tying a red ribbon around the skin.

You're mine, she said. Her lips were small drawing in the wrinkles from the outside. The poppies of the field were in her fingers, a field of wheat pale pale yellow brown, the soft grass came up with long stiff hairs, she felt each individual one as it passed by her swollen lip. Mary Bell, she called. The voice was faint and far away. The house was behind and all those people gone. Her friend was serenely walking, the child followed, his arms filled with the wild flowers they had picked. She saw the floating edges of the gown, on the slope of the hill they lost their footing, fell and tumbled rolling down the incline in the direction of the sea. She held her breath to see them rise again.

Her eyes were closed to feel the motion of the dance floor which rocked her back and forth. Her skin was smoothed over and soft to the touch the folds of her white nightgown came around her naked body, below her legs jerked, she held them tight and let them go. Her mother turned the corner and looked in. The wheel chair was on the road grinding through the gravel, the nodding head swollen up had been bandaged down over the lack of hair, the voice pulled out by the bushes as they went past, threads from the weave of her suit were shredded on the twigs and leaves. The stiffness suddenly gone, the body spilled out and emptied, the contents were strewn on the ground. She sucked up the entire affair and spat it out again.

A large white flower opened out over the water and a green dragonfly hovered over the middle. The wings ceased to beat and it fell into the center, the long thin papery tail shimmered in the water. She would be disheveled just at the time when the women around would whisper and point. Talking to her neighbor, the ceremony would be short. In a small community like this, that sort of thing doesn't go unnoticed.

It comes so easily on a hot summer's day. Have you seen the delicious green of our meadow? Soft. I just love the country air. Something fresh. Have you seen our flowers? The men are particularly complimentary especially today. A special day. Today there was a smile, her mouth was wide and welcoming. Today she was coy and still. She walked back to the house touching each plant good-bye.

A caress. Give me my due, she said. Her arms had encircled all that she could see. She cut a rose to smell and held it out to her friend in the seat beside her. It takes away the odor, she said, when it's too close. Always in the handbag for those moments. She spoke about the weather. It hadn't rained during most of the summer and the lawns in the yards were burnt.

She swept back and into her room to open the windows wide, to throw out the old flowers and there was her husband so small a reduced person walking on the lawn, forcing his way among the stiff blades of grass. She watched in fury. Off, she screamed, off. That's no place for you at this time. This instant.

The little figure ran hither and thither darting to get away, its speed increased as it covered the extent of the lawn.

No face, she said, at least show me your face.

It was big round grown tight with fat and with one more breath she saw it shrink down and collapse. So small.

More careful, she cried. You have to be more careful.

The tiny face was wrinkled but quiet. She put a hand out of the window to touch the lip. The day was very cold, she took a sweater from the drawer to wrap around her shoulders. The hurried man had gone, the lawn was empty. She watched in vain for him to reappear. Her hand trembled on the sill, a long fly landed close and walked across the white paint.

There's no one there, she called. No one?

Back in the bed, her body was wrapped in sheets her face shone out with pleasure the window burst inward and through her hair she felt the rush of the clouds and the wind which brought in the outside. The vacuum in the room had gone, the sun moved in and stood over her bed, close to her grasp close to her fingertips. There: the yellow disk that browned her skin. She ran her hands down the length of her legs to feel the warmth and heat.

The silent house with the sun on the inside, her husband gone and a dance last night. Her voice echoed in the room, in the haze and the hot sun her faint smile appeared.

Isn't it lovely dear? The countryside. I couldn't repeat it too many times, especially to someone like you. The garden is very close. Fix it up nice, will you dear, when I'm gone? Take it for my own. My own.

She was frightened and straightened her back to take away

the cramps. She would wait for one more cloud to disappear.

In a minute the rain will stop and we'll be able to go out. You have no idea what a treat you are in for.

She took the young man by the arm. I'm just crazy about gardens and nature. There's something fresh and green. Wistful, that's my nature. A bit shy and even coy. Have you seen the clouds, they move so fast. You won't mind.

Swaying in the wind, a leaf, a cloud, a piece of grass, the bird in the sky. They all fitted nicely into her cage. She hung it by the window. The remains which she wished to be seen, the things that she liked, lovely lovely things that would rest behind, a small moon cut out of paper pasted on the wall, a lock of her hair, something of herself to wrap the dry flowers. For all those who hadn't understood. She had brought the gilded cage the other day. All for my men she thought.

They danced together. Just one last dance, a waltz if that's what you like? She rotated around, the music faltered as they turned until they barely moved. She made her apologies, I do have to go. Whirling away without the music, whirled to her cage, her disdainful look opened the door, she stepped in her speed on a plant crushed it with her heel, ripped and tore, an angry eye grew in her head large and then larger, she pushed her way in. It's my right, it's mine.

An eye growing on a stalk, a round bubble with a lens, she held her breath to see the view. The window curved in a hollow, the mouth that kissed the eyelids was swollen, the yellow glare came through an opening surrounded by torn flesh and the vapor floated away in the wind.

She pulled everything up behind, the carpet of the earth by the roots wrapped in the sheets, curled in the ball that grew around and pressed into the pane to wait. The sleep would come filling the gap. She peered out in the glare to the room whereas she danced, the rows of figures came one by one to take her hand and eye, to whirl her off for an allotted amount of time. They washed the sphere and placed it back pushing the bulging surface through the square hole.

The speed slowed her heavy limbs, losing the strength to see out she slipped down the rounded sides to the bottom, the light passed over her head leaving her below. Pinned down, warm and cosy she was unable to walk across the room to look out the window. Her head was crowned with garlands of flowers, picked she thought by cupids. They were running behind the bushes and under the trees picking in their chubby fists bunches of wild flowers deep blue to match her dress. Flecks of color in their fists, flecks of color in her hair drifting out and spinning around, a little light bubble rising from the foam in the sea a feather resting on the ground picked up by the slightest breath of wind and carried further on.

The rounded sphere grew and left her inside, the angry surface was far away expanding into the fields she couldn't see, pushing its red network and blind lens through the world behind. The shapes and shadows were no longer focused on the back of the eyeball, lost the colors whirled in her head, burned in a fire they vanished from sight and turned to black. The screen was dark, stretching her hands curled and uncurled they bumped the cupids' wings, brushed her fingers through their feathers took their mouths with hers. Their soft bodies, round legs and arms slid alongside lay beside her no longer moving. The night and the sheets mingled in her hands, she walked lightly on tiptoe drifting downward, the black night opened up, there was more and more surface to be covered. She rubbed by, her hands running over the smooth line and hung on to her dream until the long fall melted in her head and the space beyond froze in the tracks. The blue shadows on the snow glittered by her side, the pain of the cold burnt, in a sudden acceleration that she hadn't expected she let go and disappeared.

CHAPTER X

The weather would be clear but hot, the morning mist was almost gone, a few white patches lay close to the forest over the meadow. The sun was beginning to melt the grass and the earth underneath. In the center there was a slight depression, he thought he saw the fluid bubbling in the heat. Good to suck tasting the end of his fingers, the ladies nodded their heads and straightened their hats rocking in their chairs to pass the time of day.

It wasn't at all expected.

Dead like that, like Mrs Simon.

Walking over the day before, they wound their faces up tight, pitched forward, one eye watched another.

Step carefully he suggested shaking his head. The ground would boil over in front of their eyes. You don't want to wake up what lies in the ground. His grandmother knew. You should have asked her first. She'd tell you what you wouldn't suspect lying cold frozen in the winter and thawing out in the spring and summer. Those thoughts that had died, she was always mumbling in his ear. His heart beat rapidly, just when you thought they had gone, tears came to his eyes, they come pushing up through the soil into the root hairs of the plants pulled up toward the sky and out they go in the sun drifting away. Close your mouth before it's too late, she always said.

The last shreds of mist had disappeared.

They say it was her divorce.

Did you see her at the party? Disgraceful.

Couldn't get enough I suppose.

His lips were white and he put his fingers in his ears, but then she didn't stop either. An incessant voice.

And the grandmother carried right on.

Strong as an ox it seems.

In the early morning he had tiptoed in. The top of the sheets was warm from the sun that had just come in the window. He had meant to be quiet, to say nothing at all. The plant on the table breathed in his ear, he gasped for air. The smell was stronger than he had expected and the heat that accumulates during the night and drifts out from the nightgown was no longer there. The face was turned to the wall, her skin was cold. His finger ran through the dust on the table surface, the room was shut up not to be used and he closed the door.

The outside air was cool, the lawn still a little damp. His ears were red around the rims. Perhaps the lady in yellow would speak next.

Never mind, she said.

He put his hand up to her chin and pushed.

Careful.

He pushed until he heard the vertebrae crack in the back. That's the way it happens. He put his hand in the mouth avoiding the teeth and thrust back. The gills opened wide, flared out under the pressure, he made a snapping noise with his tongue and the body relaxed. The chair fell over backwards and the loose head hit the floor and splintered. He tickled the feet that stuck up in the air and laughed for the lady.

Never mind.

The ladies giggled, covering their mouths to stifle the noise. They picked up the yellow doll and straightened its clothes, talking again among themselves. He strained his ear to hear what they said.

The voices rose and fell beyond his reach, murmuring whispers that came to him in his sleep from behind the wall. The flies circled above his head all through the night landing on the walls and lamp, letting go and circling again, buzzing fanning their wings. He could dream by himself, but the woman spoke in his ear and her tongue worked its way around the rim tickling the soft hairs. A hand touched his brow. The moon was full, the white light shining on the floor and the wall. The night sky was cloudless, the trees and lawn were pale and still.

He asked about the tears.

You wash them out, boats for the bathtub and a sponge for his back. She leaned over to scrub, they'll be cooler that way, don't let them suffer in the heat. There's a chill in the mountain streams and in the freshness of the pine forest. The woman next door filled a pail, nudging away the tiny cats wobbling to her shoes on the cold cement floor. Get on about your business, she told him. Don't you come around here looking for nothing. The dust swirled around her ankles, bits of fur floated in the icy water. A light bulb as he turned to look shone on the grey metal beaded with sweat reflected in each drop and her heavy red face emitted a heat that prickled his own. The round circle of the full moon was broken and stretched on the turbulent surface, pulled out into long pieces squeezed and pushed broken again by the floating fur that didn't reflect the light. The water calmed and flattened, at his hand below, the swollen moon shone in his window, he could reach down in the cold and in the sky. As he watched she turned over the bucket with her foot pouring it out, the last drop fell. In the dark the damp bodies were lifted out on the end of a shovel and taken out in the garden to be buried.

That's good fertilizer, she whispered hoarsely in his ear, of the first grade.

The roots inserted themselves around and into the skin that lay intact and whole, plants pushed up towards the sun. The first leaves came out in the heat, the cold green surface warmed and divided into several lobes. The carcasses were emptied as he lay on the ground, the roots in the muscles, bowels and brain moved them up to strengthen the stem, the final dregs transported up to the tip he waited for the flowers to appear. The good woman had left, she fussed inside her house dusting and sweeping. He laughed under the hot blue sky and pulled with his eye the flower out to its greatest size, the red petals came flat and soft velvet to the touch. The breeze started up and gently moved the leaves and the flower taking off the vapors.

In the full summer white hairless worms turned in the thinness of the leaf twisting at the surface, redoubling and working back to the succulent heart. When they had finished and gone away he took down the end product, a thin network of veins which he held up to the sky dividing the blue into tiny irregular sections. The lacework spread under his touch, the leaf took on gigantic size expanding like a net over the billowing mounds of vegetation.

He called with delight, the blue sky and wind were in his head blowing through the veins and arteries bared to the sky, growing in the field like grass multiplying heads he bent around to look through and was cut by the ladies who passed, gathered up in bunches and taken inside.

There was nothing in the bed, he said to no one in particular, but the tiny inside shell, the husk of a seed. I ate the seed.

And the child, they said, browned over and burned. She had a careful hand.

Those women who talk so much.

Mrs Sterne had swelled during the night to the size of the house, filled up with a fluid that broke in the morning when they opened the door.

The world is a merry place for you, she said. Stella was sweeping the downstairs. As your mother used to say the roses come out each morning and shine their bright red lights into your eyes. She swept the dust out onto the front walk.

Beating on the window in the morning, beating the petals against the glass trying to get in.

He landed in the water with his feet in the air caught like a cork in the flowing stream. His laughter bubbled up. Look Mother, no hands. He swung in the currents moving up in the warmth and down in the cold, going out with the tide. Up above the blue sky was clear, below the water was sunlit right down to the bottom. He waved to his mother as he passed her by on the bridge.

Is that my son floating in the water on such a day? A bright sun and I can see all the fish from here.

She leaned over and he went out to sea. Her figure became smaller, a blotch of color fastening down her hat shaded from the sun.

Out to sea rolling in the swell he came in for a landing and was sucked out again in the back wash of the waves. Up on the crest he could see the figures walking on the vast expanse of beach picking up shells, shot back in he rolled over on the sand, the sea at his back running in and running out the gulls turning overhead.

There's no one here, he told an early visitor, but you could look upstairs.

With the low tide he walked along the sea, the broken shells under his feet cut through the skin drawing blood from the bottom that was diluted to pink and drawn away by the salt water. He filled his basket with shells, down the line the beach was charged with leaping ladies splashing in the ocean kicking their heels. Had they never seen the water before? He straightened his tired back. They giggled in front of their husbands. It's the water that entices them tickles them as they playfully put their toes in and take them out with tiny screams of delight and horror.

I see you, he called, you silly women.

Their hats nodded in the breeze, white feathers leaned over the rims and hung before their eyes, they waddled through the water among themselves and left their husbands playing cards on the sand.

He pulled them in on long lines, caught in the runout they struggled until the thrashing figures went into the hole of his eye, the world turned black as they cut out the light and the sea, their strangled voices called from the back of his throat.

My dears, he said, it's without hope. There's no other way to win.

The splashing had ceased, a small voice whispered, she's with us here. I'm holding her hand.

In the darkness his hand went up to his face and he felt his closed eyes.

In there among you all?

A faint voice came through his teeth, you might of seen which one she was. Lace borders on her yellow blouse. Mixed up with us by mistake.

And if I cry?

Did you expect us to drop out one by one?

He tasted salt in his mouth and felt the streaks on his face.

The spray from the sea was drifting on the wind carried inland, the grass and trees turned brown.

At night tucked in his bed he heard the sounds come up from downstairs. He waited in the darkness, his eyes opened and fixed on the ceiling. The door to the room was opened a crack but the light in the hall was dim. He leaned over the side of the bed and called out, the guests were talking and drinking.

My dear those flowers look lovely on the mantelpiece.

He heard her laughter spring up, rushing toward the flowers and into the vase. The water bubbled, air breaking out at the surface, the stems stiffened the guest looked away and the voices ceased.

No longer there? I couldn't be more sorry. She held his hand and helped him off the fence.

I can call you anytime?

His hand went out toward the sky and the field that stretched in front of the house. He touched the line between the blue and the green and drew his finger across it. The paint smudged, smeared. The water in his eye washed against the surface. A tree rotated upside down and rightside up, the horizon came back and steadied, he called again and again until he was told to stop.

You make me nervous. Stella was working hard.

Hold my heart, he said, gay as a bird. Low in the water he was propped up by a hand under his belly. Free floating for a moment he tried a few strokes. She came and chased him away with the broom.

The dust got into his face and stung his eyes, the voices were low held down by the fire that grew in his mind. The heat came from far away much hotter than he had imagined burning the wall paper down the corridor. It curled up scorched black rolling into long cylinders at the base of the wall. Disappearing behind a line of red and yellow the hot steam and smoke bent what he could see, a door shimmered undulating in the heat and collapsed with the strain, the wall gave way bricks shooting out to the side, the noise smothered by the roar. The light near the floor rolled into a ball, the leaves growing by his hand had turned to ash.

A pleasant voice came across the room, I've always been a friend of hers. Isn't it terribly hot in here, she pulled out her handkerchief. Stuffy, and brings the flies in.

Today, he said, I'm not bored.

The long hours of summer were burning away, the ceiling was low. Stella was closing the windows. He looked out from behind the curtain to see the black clouds rolling up on the horizon. It's raining over there, he called, coming closer.

The wind took up the first trees, the heat blocked in the house was beginning to dissipate, a pane rattled in a gust that flattened the grass and turned over the leaves on the bushes near the house. His nose was pressed to the window, she was pulling down the shades.

The sound of his heart in the chest moved under his hand, running hard in the excitement. He was lost in the wave. It came even harder, the wind swept up the rain and carried it straight in.

Someone took his arm and his furious face ripped in the wind falling into rain beating on the windows.

What shall you do today? He noticed a curious expression.

The day broke around him the light came through the clouds and the weather lifted so that he could see across the field.

Shall we sit together and wait until someone comes?

He plays by himself they said, there isn't much you can do.

Happy now? He produced a large tear that grew in size in the corner of his eye. It hovered waiting to run over and down his cheek.

Is your grandmother well?

He didn't know.

They say she's become strange.

His angry stare cleared the air, and a silence replaced the buzzing tongues.

Such a serious face, the one he has. He hit back with his fist and removed the blemish.

When the day was over he went out the front door and walked toward the field. The sound of the voices that came from the house disappeared. He could hear the night insects, the breathing of his dog. Her face? He turned around and looked at the moon which lay behind throwing a pale light on the facades of the darkened houses that led down the road. Casting forth the light from his eyes into the mirror, the white globe sat behind the glass the shadows and craters dim and obscure. The cold light fell on the paving stones, he leaned down to look more closely and it continued on its way. Above the trees the sky was lit up with the pale glow, no stars behind. The flocks of birds that gathered in the fall were circling above the trees their black forms darkening the shadows and the bright sky.

The voices held their tongues, the women stood apart and watched. A hand went up to a mouth and held it tight, he smiled in answer with the corner of one lip, his laugh echoing back into his ears, he watched their flesh and bones the muscles underneath the skin, soft female muscles with rounded sides. The whirring sounds attracted his attention, he plunged in his hand grasped the mechanism and it fell apart.

The expression changed in the face that was opposite.

You're my only one. Your eyes, nose, ears and skin. Gently now careful of my preparation.

She was putting on her hat. It was tied carefully under her chin with a bow. A sun hat with floppy edges.

I'm going out dear, to get some sun.

He waved his hand.

Under the influence of the pale moon she went out with the tide. The whirling walking people dressed in black clambered over him blotting out the sunlight. In the confusion he caught his face on a pin, the scratch brought tears to his eyes and torn out into the night on the wing the pain cracked in his head and his arms floated across the landscape to the line where the mountains met the plain. He cut loose the base of the mountain slitting open the thin land and reached for the woman stepping carefully on the mirror. His hand would hit the glass just as she knotted the bow tying down the hat under her chin.

He came through on the path of the moon, he came out the door during the night, the clouds stood in front of the moon the light bursting around the brightened edges. It hung in his bedroom during the day, it flooded the ground as he walked and leaned against the pale trees shaking their branches and eating the fruit that fell to the ground: the white flesh of an apple wrapped in pale green. His hand cool and dry gave itself out, the light and shadow moved freely through.

The blue night sky, the white clouds and moon had gone by morning, the chill retreated into the forest. The sun hurt his eyes burned the edges of eyelids and melted the flesh until the sockets were left empty the endings hanging down stuck to the curved surface of the orbit oozing material that came straight out from the brain. To fill them he took the filmy lacework from out of his mother's drawer, a thin light came from his two eyes that gave him the fixed gaze of a bird.

His grandmother laughed. Bright and childlike, she said with her imbecilic smile.

They listened to the rain fall during the night and day, to the steady dripping from the eaves of the roof, the branches and leaves. The lawn was covered with pools of water, the heat of the summer gave way to the clear cool days of the fall.

CHAPTER XI

Her eyes half opened the old woman was up before the dawn, her face obscured by veils of clouds and the land that still hid the sun, her bitter hands pushed aside the covers pulling themselves into the cold. She would talk in the night, the whispered sounds called out ripping her arms through the dark, the wall around demolished the bed outside under the fading night sky, the constellations. She used their distance with her angry eye and held it up between her fingers. The fool, she said, how little did she know with her tiny lens.

The morning came the dew was still on the grass and a light breeze stirred through the gate. In the clear air the mist rose from the cold ground as the sun burned through to light her hand.

Come close and take me for my walk. The feet were gone, dust spread around over the lawn. The green shoots grew apace, bright green yellow green, the translucent color came from the sun in the back of the garden behind the trees peeking out one corner shining up all those spears of grass. The edges bright with color, light white tinged with green and whose face do you think shone out big and rosy, bright and shiny? Her daughter's eyes glowed just at the level of the ground, I hadn't expected her so early in the morning, smoking, a cigarette without any hands. The clouds came across the sky and blotted out

the light, the face faded away until only the glow of the cigarette remained in the dark and the shadows of the birds that
hopped on the lawn picking up the luminescent seeds.

The head rolled out and down the slope, bounce bounce rising up over the pebbles and rocks. She saw it when it jumped shiv-
ered and the skin held together what was shattered underneath.
There was a certain rhythm in the sounds as it gathered speed.

So clever I had never suspected a thing, watching the situa-
tion for so long lying there smoking in the leaves even in the
night when the round world was dark and the garden dim. A
whole area without definition, she had planted roses there two
years ago.

If I had walked out I would have fallen in. No sun, no moon
just the vague impression of nothing there.

Outside on the edge swinging her hand in the new light,
the grass at the rim sloping quickly toward the hole was slippery with dew. Her shoes would slide and she had fallen once
already. The space was on the left, in the corner of the garden,
her eye saw to that point and no further. Over the edge and
way at the bottom a circle of water, just to make sure she
threw in a pebble. It rolled down the incline and pitched out
into the middle dropping out of sight. The splash came way
down below. The footing was soft and when the wind blew she
could be carried away like a leaf planing over the ground into
the hole.

To the side she could put her hand on the spot touching the
corner of the skull. Above the left eye and back, the part that
expanded in the night each morning the borders were further

away. My own head and hers and she decided to fill it in.

To fill it in you have to first clean it out she was told. The hole to the side of the eye.

Her eye dropped down in and she had to use a hook to get it out, caught under a branch.

Like dropping a penny through a grating she said later. Only there was a string attached. Her grandson broke down in gales of laughter.

That was no time she said as he offered his arm to take her across the street. She bolted her food with the rest, snapped the worm in half with her beak and drove it into the ground for another. The boy doubled in back to get behind, she flicked her tail and drove him off.

The sun set in the corner of the garden and in the afternoon she could watch the small insects dancing in the slanting light. It lit up the hairs on her arm, she saw the reeds bend in the wind the eyes burned through the bush from the rose that came out yesterday. It unfolded its petals and grew on the stem, she sprayed it with water and the dark color appeared in the dust.

She's my all, the one I always had. Picked out when no one was looking.

A bird bounced on the lawn beside the bush and poking his beak up into the top he pierced a hole in the red tissue of the petal and her eye was applied tight to the round aperture.

An eye looked back. I'll have to replace those flowers. Her daughter spoke in a calm voice and the head rolled to a stop on the lawn. Bowled from the socket the eye ran along the grass right to her hand which picked up the warm moist object. The lens was opaque. It's only a question of some other illness. Walking further on she took the skull in her hands and turned the polished yellow bones in her fingers. Her skin ran over the cracks a thumb went into an orbit, she unhooked the top and looked inside. With her finger she cleared away the packed dirt and emptied it on the ground. The flocks of birds that had been roosting in the trees in the corner of the garden stood up on their legs and launched themselves into the air, the noise of their wings deafened her ears, they took off over the wall and she watched as they disappeared flying into the sun.

I'll have to send flowers. White. The white fluffy clouds she had seen last summer passed through the sky. She'll be resurrected with the scent and blown over the fields.

Clever child, the ever ready flower, holding shut its petals until the bee comes close and then in all its splendor opening out the red and yellow petals. The roses turned to brown and black. She touched the flower, one petal detached and fell on the rug. A stone flower which never lost a part.

The falling petals in the autumn dropped where no one saw them. A dry wind rushing through the forest and along the lake brought the first patches of snow. The water was picked up by the wind, blown along and the season changed. A lone duck on its way south left and on the shore the purple and yellow asters fell into the shadow at the base of the stem. She could smell the water and the snow in the rising wind, the grey clouds came in low over the trees and stayed. The sadness came, the tears. The forest was cold and empty at that time of year.

The window opened and the curtains blew through, the

doors slammed through the house as the drafts gathered power and closed the gateways.

The winter night came in without respite, the late summer light dimmed out, the slowly shrinking world filled up with snow that worked around the stiffening body. The skin was cut and she could see from where she was sitting that the stuffing was being forced out. Sawdust. It was sewed up again and buried in the garden, in the corner. Surgery would be totally unnecessary.

Sheets of rain drummed on the windows waking her from her sleep. The dark sky and wet kept her inside, the days went by, each morning the room contracted in her head and opened out in the water, paper flowers unfolding in the glass she kept by her bed.

They took her home in tears in a black cloud that had folded itself under her skin. The rain was running off the roof, on the empty bed her black hat lay beside long hat pins. As each person came up to her with their words of sorrow she took their cold hands. The bird on the wing moved through the sky down to the sea swell tilted over the spray and foam. She ran with the wind pulled through the rain, her angry face pouted in the mirror, it's just as well that they're gone. She touched her nose, underneath the cartilage disguise were the outlines of the bone.

The other side of the room cleaned and dusted by the nurse stood behind her back, she turned and peopled the empty space, at the end of the garden the flowers were there for her to cut. In the exhaustion of the pace she stopped on the side of the road and waited for a passer-by, no face appeared to loom on the horizon to roll along the road. A harvest moon rose up in the east to replace the setting sun, its size dwarfed the trees and the road across the valley. The small figures walking home from work silhouetted against the light came into view.

The curtains that moved in the night snapped in the wind, the bones cracked in her fingers. With wet eyes her hands gathered the flowers that came from her garden fresh bouquets, water dripping from the stems she held them forward, fell under, rolled and came up. Washed and bathed in the sea walking out and dried off, rubbing vigorously the cold air held up the body, the blue line of the sea had moved, the wind had darkened the water far out to sea.

Not thought about, in case you supposed I knew. Disturbed once? Probably not. Shut the door and disappeared. Left to wait. The morning was long but then the tears would come and came, even for such a fool and she cried in the church.

CHAPTER XII

He went to see his grandmother brought there to talk to play at her feet in the heat and quiet of an afternoon.

He took his head in his hands with the neck sealed over. I thought I would see, he began bravely, how it would grow. I dreamt of such lovely things that would come up and blossom from under the ground. Daisies for your garden, tulips for the border.

Touching the small hand that trembled on the arm of the chair, he turned his head sideways and focused an eye on the rug where the faded stitch was filled with dust.

Her attention attracted by the riveted gaze she saw the early bird snatch the worm. The flower there is quite abstract. Her nostalgic eye nourished the weave with the tears that fell each night.

He struck between the red and the blue, the head bobbed up and down as the beak was forced through between the stitch. Tearing at the colors he brought up the threads pulled them free, they reeled and turned in his grasp.

Turned to worms in the back of the eye, she said don't waste your time in the grass roots and the flowers. She saw the underworld filled with a life that crawled and sucked drawing the blood out of the sky leaving only the husks behind, holding its shape for a time and then from underneath rotting away.

He had a cold beady eye with stiff feathers surrounding the rim, a robin's eye. Moist shiny but not a tear and likely not. I see you child hopping on those two feet stabbing after their tails.

She carried him across the field under her strong arm, his legs kicking behind. It was early evening, the grass came up to her waist colored dark yellow brown in the dusk. The sun had set behind, the sky was cloudless, the deep red graduated through a light green to a dark blue overhead. A cool night wind came over the long field. She gripped him tighter and they stopped together in front of the gate. The boy ran to the grill attached his arms and looked through.

Your mother's there all done up, she said.

His feathers were squeezing through the grill fluffed out on the other side. In the warm sand he would make his nest hollowing down in.

The cold day darkened. Right there quite by mistake. She stared in, her tears would turn away blown off by the chilly wind, stilled a hand at the eye and brushed the mouth. Not while I'm still alive. Run boy and she chased him through the fields. Out of breath out of mind. We'll pick some flowers from the field.

They walked among the stones.

Your poor mother, a daisy from the field and flowers from the shop, hot house flowers covered with steam from behind the glass. You would have liked that. She put the flowers on the grave and pulled up her spreading stomach gone slack with old age.

A late thrush called from the woods, a liquid sound rolling on the night wind, soft and chilling in the minor key, its dusky throat hidden among the leaves.

Would that touch you, she asked? A bird song. Not I suppose.

Clear: each stem of grass, each leaf. The trees in the forest glowed in the afterlight, the night sky bright. They could dance together the boy and the old woman each in the head of the other springing up and down on the tufts of grass, jumping on the thin ice. With the cold the monotonous cadence of the grasshoppers and crickets broke off.

Hold, she cried, hold and swing. Their feet were in the air spun outwards, the speed forced out the wrinkles and they laughed together. Spinning on a grave young and old to the tune of the thrush concealed in the woods. The moon was on the eastern horizon, the stars fading in the new light.

Above the forest he looked again, the moon was pale a telescope would bring it to his eye to fill the diameter of the lens blown up in his head, he moved over to the stars in their black space leaving it behind. The earth turned beneath his feet. The night sky damped out the noises that proliferated during the day. He emptied out his own name into the darkness, his grandmother waited angry shouting.

Gone already? Cry, she demanded.

He looked into the old face, stammered and held up the head to the moon. Hung up, reflecting the light in the dark. No tear, no smile, set. He shoved it further into the sky, pushing it in with his fist, iced.

She emptied the basket, throwing out all the old flowers, the stems had rotted. The winter outside cleared the fields, the fall flowers had gone.

Swinging on an imaginary flower she hung on the petal

sewed back on colored by the bright sun she had put in the sky. Her own moon a clear disk shone in her face she touched his hand. He moved away.

Burns your hand?

She winked in his eye.

He saw the cold fire of the firefly, her image floated by his head.

Her eye moved in searching for his in the dark, they heard the thrush for the last time as the night settled around them, the moon was higher in the sky. She was on him with her cry, in her pain her hour crowded into one glance she felt the warmth that had left the soil rising in her body. The cold draft came out of her lungs, the candle wavered and went out.

She said so.

There's no candle.

No, there's no candle. Not in the middle of the field. Or did you bring one?

Her face was wrinkled and tired. She reached for his hand to take him away. A diversion for a rainy day. She could rest and catch her breath sitting on a chair while he waited for a moment all in her head all in her room with the window on the garden. She would write a note and send flowers. Keep him there until she came to see him. The roots would hold.

Give me your hand and we'll go back there's nothing more to do here. Attached to the grill he was staring inside. She took his arm and led him away, the moment had passed and her pain was gone, the end of the meadow stood up again in the back of her eye. The cold draft was shut off by a closed window.

Happy now, she asked and clinging to the hand that she found at her side they rushed through the night under the moon back to the house. His feet rose up with the speed, their faces were scratched and bleeding.

He was on another tack, his shining face projected among the stars moving in their wake, his eye fixed on the foliage and grass, in slow motion he reached to pick what he saw. He wandered away in the sunlight and was sitting in a field. She followed after.

Perhaps I'm busy, he said with mild surprise.

She was thinking of a brisk walk on Sunday. We could have a row. Such a handsome face, her finger traced its lines as she grew quiet.

He wasn't looking. The grandmother nodded in her turn and walked off. She had taken his eye with her carrying it wrapped in tissues in her bag.

A passer-by commented on the empty socket, the other flared out racing away alone slowing down on the road he stopped in the country on a clear day, the sun hot on his back beating down on the field.

The grandmother walked in her garden burying her tulip bulbs. The ground was turned over, the holes were dug as she pointed her finger toward the soil. She'd always said they would come up from the roots of her brain.

He took the small head of his grandmother in his hands the tiny bones pushed in through the skin. She babbled from the corner pointing to the light that came over the wall, the backs of the fields were washed over with paint, the sun behind his head lit the line of trees and little figures that walked so far away. A piece of grass flared up in his face, the church bells were brought on the wind from over the fields and echoed in his ear racing in the flesh around the circuits until he too swung in the wind.

Her neck was twisted sideways revealing the implanted vessels flowing next to the muscle, the slow pulse that fed the brain no longer lifted the skin.

He ran his hands over the surface of the earth, the moon had gone over the crest of the hill, the night sky was filled with stars and swiftly moving clouds. The air moved along the ground of black, flat sheets that swirled around his legs. His grandmother's laugh came in with his tears, his mother lay on the bed. No laugh from her, her angry stare caught him unawares, her slow smile reached for the inside and brightened up her paint. She walked along pruning the flowers preparing the ground hopping over the grass throwing back her head, he was deafened from the center. In his head the stars appeared the laugh was carried away by the night wind. It echoed from far away the bed creaked as his mother moved and spoke his name.

Running in the field he could laugh in the end catching his breath he ran to get close to put out his hand to touch the wall. His grandmother poked her head over the top with curls in her hair, fair to the side and dyed at the back. He touched the stone and the lady, silent, made gestures from far away under the trees fading into the shadows of the forest. A leaf vibrating in the breeze that came with the light of the sun jumped on its tether fluttered on the glass. Running in the eye racing on the ground he stepped outside the door into a bright sunlit day, the grass was wet with dew, the beads of water glistened on the stems.

Opening up for the next day, the curtains blew out the window the sun unfolded, under the bed the curls of the grandmother rolled in the dust. Her burgeoning flowers brightly colored within, the petals falling off and floating down. He held her hand to pass the days proceeding slowly by.

I imagine dear that you too will go.

The falling stars had their day, she cut out a flame in the atmosphere. Her words glittered on the table and in the air, the highly polished silver had been fashioned into leaves and fruits, he stood by and picked them up. Standing in the receiving line she shook hands and looked each person straight in the eye.

I brought your curls, he said, they'd fallen under the bed. For a wig. Would her voice never stop? Ringing in his ear, blowing on his cheek. From the bed she counted the seconds as they passed on the clock. The minute hand turned in his eye as he waited, a frothing foaming liquid came out red sticky and clotted on the skin. The drenched sheets were sterilized and made ready for another, during the night the men swept up the dust for the start of the next day. Those who love and those who don't, the imploring faces looked out the windows their eyes already opaque, his own thin figure, the mouth without its nerves an unfed muscle that as he watched began to waste.

Snapped and undone, he bowed his head. The skull had been laid bare, the flowers were on the ground the earth still sticking to the roots, the mind exposed he ran along the fibers. The clouds gathered to rain far across the plain, shafts of mist falling from the sky. The brief spring came to life. The wind that blew was moist and warm. His eye touched on the road ahead and he saw in every rose that hung by her side, and on the grass that grew up from the lawn the light from his own eye.

The empty winter came in over the wall, the leaves rushed out from the eye spewing onto the ground brown and wrinkled. The clouds moved in rising from the land falling back in rain. She walked alone and vanished over the wall, the chrysanthemums bloomed high in the corner.

His ears were swollen by the cold, gone in the night he waited for the dawn that would come within the hour. Over his head and across the field the rays of sunlight flashed, in his eye flooded and filled with light, the morning mists rose off the ground, a painted moon was left in the blue sky. In the window came the scent of the flowers brought in on the hot breeze, the clouds billowed up rising on some wind that he couldn't see. He went out to catch the falling petals, to gather up those flowers that he had seen fall from her hand as she walked by in the evening. He saw the open mouths that talked, talked in their beds while dying, the leaves carried on the wind whirled and scattered, the dry tissues breaking up crushed under his feet, moving away the voices fell behind until only the faint murmur came on the wind which began to die at the close of the day. The blue sky in the day hid the stars he would see at night and the sun set at the end of the day rolling under the curved horizon.

The light from the window spread out on the floor, the

shadows were cast by the sun, the line of the sea broke into the sky. The garden that burst with flowers lost its scent, the rose that his grandmother fixed in his lapel withered away and disappeared beneath the soil.

In the bright green landscape the white clouds swung on the horizon, the dark sky was filled with stars that opened out beyond the blue night and the morning to come seen with his hand and seized by the laughter that rolled in the hills under the clouds of the storm that came with the daylight moving down the slopes of the meadows. The color was brightened by the rain, darkened by the clouds, the leaves raked up and burnt he went out in the cold, the snow turned black beside the road cluttered with footprints. The sky was grey filled again with snow and driving wind carrying with it the cries of people walking by themselves, talking to themselves the sounds of those people who talked as they died, talked and whispered smiled in their sleep walking with their eyes open during the day.

Sarah Plimpton is a painter and a poet. She divides her time between New York City and France. Her poems and prose have appeared in the New York Review of Books, The Paris Review, and the Denver Quarterly among other magazines. A collection of poems has been translated into French, L'Autre Soleil, and published by Le Cormier, Belgium. Her paintings and artist's books are in various museum collections including the Whitney Museum of American Art, the Museum of Fine Arts, Boston, and the Metropolitan Museum of Art.

How we got our name

…from *Pleasure Boat Studio*, an essay written by Ouyang Xiu, Song Dynasty poet, essayist, and scholar, on the twelfth day of the twelfth month in the renwu year (January 25, 1043):

"I have heard of men of antiquity who fled from the world to distant rivers and lakes and refused to their dying day to return. They must have found some source of pleasure there. If one is not anxious for profit, even at the risk of danger, or is not convicted of a crime and forced to embark, rather, if one has a favorable breeze and gentle seas and is able to rest comfortably on a pillow and mat, sailing several hundred miles in a single day, then is boat travel not enjoyable? Of course, I have no time for such diversions. But since 'pleasure boat' is the designation of boats used for such pastimes, I have now adopted it as the name of my studio. Is there anything wrong with that?"

Translated by Ronald Egan